Tar Baby

Tammy Campbell Brooks
Tahirah Jessalyn Brooks

Tar Baby

Author: Tammy Campbell Brooks
Tahirah Jessalyn Brooks
Title: Tar Baby
Subject: fiction
African American
Publishing 2018
Paradeyez Books
ISBN-13:
978-1732276833
Library of Congress Control Number: 2018965048

Table of Contents

Contents

Tar Baby

Introduction

In society, young black girls are constantly told that in order for them to be considered "beautiful" they have to be *light* skinned. If you are dark-skinned, then you are marginalized, and are harshly judged and ridiculed.

Tar Baby discusses issues, such as racism, colorism, self-hate, and other stereotypes that plague the black community. Self-hate begins at a very young age, and it surrounds us through imagery. Imagery is powerful because it attacks the subconscious, depicting black as evil and white as everything that is *good*.

Tianna, the main character in Tar Baby, grew up in a household where she was called derogatory names due to her skin color. In effect, that caused her to have issues within herself growing up. As Tianna got older, she began to realize the beauty of being dark-skinned, and embraced her inner and outer self.

Tar Baby is dedicated to all the dark-skinned girls who have been put down because of colorism. We know your stories and struggles. We encourage you to always find beauty from within, and not look through society's eyes to define yourselves.

Your melanin be poppin' and don't you forget it!

Tar Baby

To **A**lways **R**emember you're **B**lack **A**nd **B**eautiful the way **Y**ou are!

Chapter One

Dear Diary (In my sixth grade year)

I had fun today at school with my best friend, Tasha. I met Tasha on the first day of kindergarten in Mrs. Brown's class. Tasha and I have a lot in common. We are goofballs and we enjoy joking in class. Hehe.

Tasha and I were being made fun of today by a group of kids during lunch. Kids at my school always call us names such as, Blacky, Darkie, and Tar Baby. I hate those names.

"Tar Baby! Get down here and pick up your stuff," Tianna's mother said.

Tianna's mother, Bernadette, was a recovering alcoholic. A reformed unfit mother who didn't take care of her. She got pregnant with Tianna at the age of seventeen and had to drop out of high school. Tianna's father, Tyrone, whom Tianna called Deadbeat, never acknowledged Tianna in any way, shape, or form. She didn't have support from either of her parents. Her only support was her friend, Tasha Norwood.

Tianna was ridiculed because of her dark skin and thought of as an inferior and unruly, ugly child. She was far from unruly and ugly. She was a sweet, well-mannered, highly intelligent little girl with the most sincere smile. Her beautiful chestnut skin matched her dark beaded eyes to perfection. Tianna had dark eyelashes and to-die-for thick, naturally arched eyebrows.

She didn't get her looks from her parents.

Bernadette was light-complexioned with hazel eyes and curly hair. Her hair didn't need a relaxer and came down to her bra strap.

Tyrone resembled the basketball player Stephen Curry. He was light, bright, and damn near white. When he'd get mad, he'd turn red as a strawberry, except there was nothing *sweet* about him.

Tianna didn't know what Bernadette saw in Tyrone because neither was cut from the same cloth. They couldn't stand each other and fought about everything, even things that had nothing to do with their daughter.

Tyrone often accused Tianna of not being his daughter because she was hella dark and didn't look like him or any of his family members. According to him, he couldn't make *tar babies*.

His support mentally, physically, and financially was limited. He was basically dead.

Tianna longed for a father and mother like Tasha's parents. Tasha's father, Adonis, was a great father. He married Tasha's mother after they graduated from high school. They were middle school sweethearts who met in the sixth grade in English class.

Adonis was a captain in the military with a medical degree and would retire in a few years. Tasha's family lived in an upscale suburban neighborhood with lots of trees, hills, and green landscapes. The entire neighborhood kept their properties well maintained. During the fall, you would see neighbors outside with hefty trash bags and rakes, raking leaves from their lawns. The families had enough income to hire landscapers, but many enjoyed the outdoors and did most of their own yard work.

The neighborhood was a small tight-knit community and everyone knew each other and knew whose kids were whose. So if you were to get in trouble, you were in deep trouble, not only with your parents but the whole neighborhood. There were no secrets in this small community. Everyone raised each other's kids in this village.

When Tianna visited the Norwoods, they treated her like family. She was invited to all parties and holiday gatherings.

Tasha's mother, Sharon, could throw down in the kitchen. She cooked like she had a home full of children, but Tasha and her brother, Jackson, were the only children in the Norwood household.

Jackson was one year older than Tasha. They had a love-hate relationship. Jackson often teased Tasha and Tianna about their skin color and exclaimed how they needed to stay out of the sun before they disappeared in the nighttime.

Jackson loved teasing Tasha and Tianna, but he often protected them at school against bullies.

Tianna went downstairs to pick up her books and shoes, and ran back upstairs to put them away in her room. She sat down on her bed and turned on the TV to watch cartoons until her Grandma Debby called her from the living room.

"Tianna, come on and let's comb out your hair."

Grandma Debby lived with Tianna and her mother, and she worked as a librarian. She often brought books home for Tianna to read. She had to read one book every two to three weeks to keep her reading and comprehension skills above her sixth grade level.

Grandma Debby got the grease and the comb and began to comb out Tianna's hair.

"Grandma?"

"Yes?"

"Why can't I comb my own hair and wear it down like all the other girls at school?"

"Girllll, you ain't got them white folks' hair like them people at your school. And you tried fixing your hair before, and it was a mess."

"I always have my hair braided; why can't I let my hair be free?"

"Your hair is not pretty enough to be worn down. Your hair gets matted and it's hard to manage. We need to get you a relaxer soon."

"What's a relaxer?"

"It's a chemical treatment so that your hair can be prettier and more easily managed."

Tianna had always wanted to wear her hair down despite what anyone thought about it. She didn't care what other people were going to say about her or her hair. It was a part of her identity.

"I just want to wear my hair down for once, Grandma. I don't wanna be ashamed and wear my hair up all the time."

"You know how to do your own hair yet?"

"Yes."

"No, you don't. Now be quiet, and let's get yo hair combed."

Tianna sat clenching her fists in pain while her grandma yanked the comb through her hair. When she was finally done, she wrapped it up with a scarf and told her to go to bed. Tianna was so upset about the talk she had with her grandma, she stomped into her room and slammed the door. Her mom heard the door slam from downstairs and came rushing to Tianna's room.

"Who do you think you are, slamming doors in this house?" she demanded.

"Grandma made me upset."

"I don't care if you're upset or not, don't be slamming doors in this household. You slam another door in this house, you getting a whooping. Do you understand?"

"Yes, ma'am."

"How did Grandma upset you anyways?"

"I want to wear my hair down to school tomorrow but Grandma won't let me."

Tianna's mom gave her a funny look and told her the same thing Grandma Debby said.

"Girl, you ain't got them white folks' hair, now quit trippin'. You don't got the straight hair like they do."

"I want to embrace my coily hair."

"When we get a relaxer in your hair, you can wear it down whenever you like. This summer we are going to the beauty salon to get you a relaxer."

"I heard that relaxers burn your scalp."

"No, they don't. Now go to sleep."

Tianna's mom turned off the lamp and closed the door on her way out. Tianna lay in her bed that night wondering was wrong with her hair and why she couldn't wear it down. She wanted to be unique and not like the other girls. She wished her mom and grandma would let her walk out of the house not having to worry about carrying a scrunchie or putting her hair up in braids. It was only a matter of time until she knew how to comb her own hair and she couldn't wait until that day. Tianna took mental abuse, not only from the kids at her school, but from her own family too.

On the last day of eighth grade, Jasmine, who most students referred to as a "mean girl," told Tianna,

"You know, you are not bad looking at all, but you would be a lot prettier if you were light skinned."

"Excuse me?"

"Girl, I didn't st-st-st-stutter. You would be *prettier* if you were light skinned."

"My skin is beautiful no matter what people think. If you don't like my skin then don't look at me."

Jasmine walked off and mumbled, "Angry Black girl."

"Hey Tianna, what's up?" Jamal asked, coming out of the gym where he'd been playing basketball.

"Oh, hey, Jamal. Nothing. I'm tired of these girls and this school. I'm ready to move on to high school and then college."

"Yeah, I feel you. Oh, by the way, I heard what Jasmine said about you, but I disagree. I think you are pretty just the way you are."

Tianna got this huge smile on her face. All thirty-two white teeth were seen and glowing like a bright star in the night. She was in awe over what had just transpired and wanted to pinch herself to make sure she wasn't dreaming. Jamal said she was *pretty*.

No one had ever called her *pretty*. She couldn't wait to tell Tasha, but she wanted to be sure.

"Jamal, you don't have to lie to me. I know that I'm not as attractive as the other girls."

"I know you are not, you are beautiful inside and out. Don't you forget that," Jamal said as he spun his basketball on his middle finger. He was a point guard for the Emerson Bobcats basketball team. He was one of the most popular boys in school. And he said that she was pretty—but not only that she was pretty, he said she was beautiful, too, inside and out.

"All right, I will see you in class."
"Bye, Jamal."

Eighth grade was finally over and now Tianna felt that something had to change. She had to toughen up and get thicker skin because the teasing was not going to end.

It would only get worse in her high school years.

Chapter Two

The bell rang for the last class period of the day. Tasha and Tianna walked down the hall surveying all the cute eleventh-grade athletes that hung in the halls talking instead of going to class. They saw Tasha's brother Jackson in the hallway.

"Get y'all fast asses to class and stop looking at boys that are not interested in y'all."

"Jackson, mind yo business and worry about Shantae. I heard that she's going to dump you soon for Jamal," Tasha retorted.

"Who told you that?"

"Nunya."

"Who is Nunya?"

"None of yo business." Tasha and Tianna burst out laughing.

"Shut up and you better not leave me waiting for you after school like yesterday. You need to be on time because I got practice today."

"Whatever, bye Jackson."

"See ya, Jackson," Tianna said in a shy surly voice as she waved Jackson away. She turned to Tasha. "Your brother is kind of cute."

"Girl, no he ain't with his big ass head. I need to buy you a new pair of glasses." Tasha laughed.

Shantae had overheard Tianna say that Jackson was "kind of cute', and walked over. She said that if Tianna had something to say about Jackson, then she needed to speak with her *first*. She told Tianna to keep her man's name out of her mouth.

Tianna didn't care for Shantae and felt that Jackson could do much better. Shantae was loud, rude, and vain. She thought that she was better than everybody. She wore the latest fashionable clothes, and her curvy body fit her outfits to perfection. She got her hair and nails done almost weekly.

She could have any man she wanted and many were waiting in line until she and Jackson were no longer a couple.

Shantae and Jackson had been dating since middle school. They broke up once, but then got back together and had been together ever since.

Jackson loved Shantae, but Tianna wasn't sure if his feelings were reciprocated, since the reason for their break-up was that Shantae had cheated on Jackson.

He forgave her and she hadn't cheated again, yet.

Shantae had always liked Jamal, but she wasn't Jamal's type of girl. Jamal's preference was humble girls, not loud mouth girls like Shantae. Jamal was reserved, intelligent, and attracted to the same type of girls.

Shantae, as much as she tried, would never be Jamal's ideal girl.

He wasn't interested in her and she knew it. And ignored many of her advancements toward him.

His rejection of her made Shantae envious of Tianna because she often saw Jamal and Tianna together. She wondered if they would be a couple.

She saw the way Jamal looked at Tianna and she longed for him to look into her eyes the same way he looked at Tianna.

She didn't know what he saw in such a darkie. Tianna was cute, but she was still a tar baby.

Jamal was infatuated with Tianna. To him, everything about her was perfect. Jamal saw her in the library reading a book and he began to daze off.

"*Tianna is so beautiful*," he thought as he looked into the eyes of a resplendent girl. He loved everything about her. Her sparkling brown eyes, her plump full lips, her beautiful Afro, her smooth chocolate skin. But most importantly, he loved her pure unique soul.

She wasn't a typical teenage girl, in fact, she was quite the opposite. She was a girl deemed "weird" or "peculiar" because of her uniqueness.

She was the type of girl you would see sitting in the back of class, afraid of others judging her. Despite what others said about Tianna, Jamal found her attractive from head to toe. He loved all her "flaws" and he loved her for who she was.

"Who are you staring at?" Curtis asked Jamal. Curtis was Jamal's best friend and he was always by his side.

"No one," Jamal said as he walked out of the library.

Curtis had noticed Jamal hanging out with Tianna a lot. Whenever he saw her he stared at her like a deer caught in headlights, and whenever he and Jamal were talking, he would bring up Tianna for some unknown reason.

Curtis followed Jamal out of the library and ran to catch up with him.

"I have a feeling that you like Tianna."

"Why do you say that?"

"Every time you see her, I catch you staring, and whenever you and I are having a conversation, you always bring her up."

"Okay, I do like Tianna. She is perfect from head to toe. I don't see why she is teased and called names. I will stand up to whoever wants to call her names and make sure that they treat her with respect. She is a queen and deserves to be treated like one."

"You should tell her how you feel."

"Nah, man. What if she doesn't feel the same about me?"

"You never know, bro. She could feel the same way, but you don't even know because you're too scared to tell her. Prom is coming up in a few weeks. You could ask her out to the prom?"

"Yeah, I'll think about it," Jamal said as he walked to his next class.

Jamal didn't know that Curtis wanted to ask Tianna out to the prom, too. He didn't want Jamal to ask her to the prom because he had a feeling that she would say "yes." So he began to think of a plan. He was going to ask her to the prom *first*.

"Tianna, you know prom is coming soon," Tasha announced.

"Yeah, I know."

"Do you want to go together? You, me, and Darren will have a good time."

"Girl, I'm not trying to be the third wheel between you and Darren."

Darren was Tasha's boyfriend, and they had been together since freshman year of high school.

Tasha and Darren were made for each other. He called Tasha his China doll because of her smooth chocolate skin, and long dark shiny silky hair that she often relaxed. Tasha did her own hair and make-up, and often did Tianna's hair too. But Tianna wasn't a huge fan of make-up; she preferred her natural beauty.

Tasha was an aspiring beautician and make-up artist, and wanted to own her own beauty salon, doing celebrities' hair and make-up before they went on stage to perform.

She once met Beyoncé when her parents lived in Houston, Texas. She talked about how nice Beyoncé was and how television didn't do her any justice because she was flawless in person. She dreamed of doing Beyoncé's hair and make-up. She would even do it for free for marketing purposes.

"Why don't you ask Jamal to take you to the prom?"

"How would I look asking Jamal to take me tothe prom? Besides, Jamal doesn't want to go with me. You know he likes those light skinned hootchies with the good hair." Tianna rolled her eyes thinking of all the girls that liked Jamal.

"Jamal isn't into hoochies and thots. Jamal is in love with you!"

"No, he's not. He sees me as a friend. Someone that he feels he needs to protect."

"Anywhoo, if you say so, but Jamal has been bitten by the Tianna love bug" Tasha teased and demonstrated a symbol of a heart with her hands and fingers.

Tasha was right. Jamal was in love with Tianna and everyone could see it, except her. How did she miss the signs? He had never dated anyone throughout high school and every girl chased him like cats in heat.

He was always cordial and nice to them all, but none of them held his interest like Tianna.

"I'm going to the basketball game to see Darren play and I know you want to go, so Jackson and I will pick you up at six-thirty tonight." Tasha didn't give Tianna a chance to decline, so she reluctantly accepted her invitation. Besides, she had no homework and didn't feel like staying home on a Friday night.

Tianna hurried home to pick out her outfit. She knew that she had to look fly since Tasha *and* Jackson were coming to pick her up.

She liked Jackson, but didn't want her best friend to know that she was interested in her brother. She didn't know if it was against the friendship guidelines to not date or have a crush on her bestie's brother. She and Tasha never had any rules, since they were as thick as thieves and tighter than a sneeze. They had each other's backs.

Searching through her closet, Tianna couldn't decide what she would wear to get and keep Jackson's attention.

She was a year younger than Jackson, and knew she had to dress like girls his age. She had a few tank tops, but her grandmother and mother didn't like her showing off her large perky breasts. They thought it would draw too much unwanted attention from the boys.

Tonight, she wanted the attention from Jackson, though. He wasn't a boy. He'd turned eighteen last month, and according to the law, that made him a *man*. But he was Shantae's man. Well, for now, Tianna thought.

She continued searching for the perfect outfit and eventually found it. She ate dinner with her family, and when she was done, she put the final touches on her hair and outfit before Tasha *and* Jackson arrived.

A car horn sounded and Tianna heard Tasha call her name.

"I'm coming," Tianna yelled from her bedroom window.

Why did Jackson have to be so damn rude honking his horn like he was always in a hurry? The game didn't start until seven p.m. and the gymnasium was only ten minutes away.

Jackson honked the horn again.

"I'm coming!" Tianna said with irritation.

Jackson honked the horn for a third time and Tianna could hear him laughing while Tasha hit him.

Tianna grabbed her jacket and put it on. She didn't want her grandmother to see her tank top cropped denim blouse. She ran downstairs in a frenzy so that Jackson wouldn't honk again and bring Bernadette outside to curse him out.

Bernadette didn't care for Jackson, and always thought he was rude. He often did things to irritate her, so her getting after him was nothing new.

"Don't you be coming in this house late, Tianna," Bernadette said.

"I won't, I will be home as soon as the game ends," Tianna assured her mother as she ran out the front door and slammed it.

"Don't be slamming my door!"

Tianna ignored her mother's demands and opened Jackson's car door only to be disappointed when she saw Shantae in the front seat.

What the hell was she doing in here? Tianna wanted to say, but instead, she gave a weak sigh and greeted Tasha, Jackson, *and* Shantae.

"Oooh, you smell and look good. Who are you looking and smelling good for? Jamal?" Jackson laughed.

Shantae gave him a smack on the right shoulder as she sucked her teeth with envy.

"Whatttt?" Jackson asked.

"Leave Tar Baby *alone*," Shantae said.

"Aye, why you still calling her that name?" Jackson wanted to know since Tianna hadn't been called Tar Baby since middle school.

"Cuz, she's still dark."

"You know, dark skinned girls are coming out," Jackson announced like it was breaking news.

"No, we *been* out. It's just that y'all knuckle heads haven't noticed," Tasha hissed as she gave Tianna a high and low five to the side and up high.

They laughed at Tasha's clap back as they drove off to the basketball game.

Once they arrived at the junior varsity basketball game, Tasha and Tianna sat together, while Jackson and Shantae sat away from them in a corner, uninterested in the game. Tasha spotted Darren, and as soon as he saw her, he went up to the bleachers where they were seated.

"Hey, babe. Good luck on your game."

"Thanks, babe. What's up, Tianna?"

"Hey, Darren. Nothing much. I'm here to see you play. Good luck."

"Thanks."

Tasha gave Darren a quick peck on the lips before he jogged toward the basketball court. A few minutes later, Tasha saw Jamal and Curtis and quickly tapped Tianna on the shoulder.

"There's Jamal!"

"Oh, hush. Like I said, Jamal's not that into me."

"Girl, yes he is. Everyone sees it but you."

Jamal and Curtis saw Tasha and Tianna and walked over to where they were seated.

"Hey, ladies. What are y'all doing here?" Jamal asked.

"We're here to watch Darren play," Tianna replied

"That's cool. You look nice," Jamal said.

"Aww, thanks."

Tianna only looked nice because she wanted to get Jackson's attention, but she didn't want Tasha, and especially not Jackson, to know.

"So, what are y'all doing after the game?" Curtis inquired.

"I'm going home because I have a curfew."

"Me too," Tasha replied.

"Cool."

"I'll be back, I gotta go pay the water man. I've been drinking too much water," Jamal said as he excused himself.

Paying the water man was Jamal's way of saying he had to go to the restroom. They all laughed because they knew what it meant.

This is my time. Curtis thought to himself. *I'm going to ask Tianna to stay after the game so I can ask her to the prom.*

Curtis waited for Jamal, and once he saw him leave, he decided to make his move.

"Tianna, once the game is over, can I talk to you about something?"

Tianna was confused. She barely knew Curtis, and the only time they'd ever talked was in math class.

"Sure," she replied.

"Cool. I'll see you after the game."

"What was that about?" Tasha asked as he walked away.

"Girl, I have no idea. I'm just as baffled as you."

Tasha shrugged and continued enjoying the game, while Jackson and prissy Shantae were in the corner cuddling and kissing. Seeing Jackson and Shantae making out made Tianna sick to her stomach. She couldn't wait until they broke up.

The game ended and Curtis told Jamal to wait in the parking lot because he was going to talk to someone. Curtis never specifically told Jamal that it was Tianna. Tianna told Tasha to wait in the parking lot as well, because she was curious about what Curtis wanted with her.

Curtis pulled Tianna to the back where nobody could see them and began stroking her arm.

"Curtis, what are you doing?" Tianna asked as she pushed his hand away from her.

"I wanted to ask you about something."

"Ask me about what?"

"You know how prom is two weeks away?"

"Yeah?"

"Will you go to the prom with me?"

Tianna was confused. She felt as though she was being set up by Jamal, or Curtis was only asking her to win a bet. Tianna barely knew Curtis and wasn't attracted to him at all. *Why is he asking me to the prom?* Tianna thought to herself.

"Sorry, Curtis, but I can't go with you."

"Why not? I know you have feelings for me—"

"Wait a minute. What?" Tianna was bewildered and placed her hand on her right hip. "Listen Curtis, you're cool, but I don't know you well enough to go to the prom with you. You transferred to my math class a week ago."

"But we talk in class, so I don't understand why you're rejecting me like this?" Curtis started to get frustrated.

"The only time we talk in class is when you need a pencil or when you didn't do your homework, and you ask for answers. That is the extent of our communication. Do you think we have a connection?"

"I actually do." *Damn it, there goes my confidence,* Curtis thought to himself.

"Well, I'm sorry and I didn't intend to mislead you. You're a cool guy, but I don't know you that well."

"I understand. My bad. Let's forget about me asking. I'll see you on Monday."

"Goodnight, Curtis."

Tianna felt bad for rejecting Curtis, but she wanted to go to the prom with Jackson or Jamal, *not* Curtis. She grabbed her denim jacket off the bleachers and walked toward the parking lot, trying to find Tasha.

Tasha rolled down the window of Jackson's car and waved her hand so that Tianna could see her. Tianna opened the car door to sit in the backseat with Tasha and Darren. She pulled out her phone and texted her mom that she would be home in about fifteen minutes.

Tianna was quiet the entire car, until she noticed that everyone in the car was staring at her. The stare down went on for about five minutes, until Tianna eventually became uncomfortable.

"What?" Tianna asked nervously.

"You're being awfully quiet," Tasha said.

"I'm just a little tired, that's all."

"So, what were you and Curtis talking about?"

"I'll tell you when we get home."

"Tell us now, we want to know." Jackson inserted his two cents into the conversation that had nothing to do with him.

"Mind yo business, damn," Shantae hissed.

"Aye, she is my business," Jackson told Shantae with a serious look on his face.

Shantae slapped Jackson's shoulder and told him to shut up. Jackson did, but only because he didn't want to make a scene in front of Tianna. He wanted to know what Curtis said to her because he would handle it.

If he was my man. I wouldn't hit him and tell him to shut up. Jackson deserves better, and once he sees me in my prom dress, he's going to think twice about being with her, Tianna imagined.

"You know you can tell us anything," Darren said.

"I know. I'm just tired, that's all."

The next few minutes were silent in the car.

"Babe, can we go to McDonald's? I want a milkshake," Shantae asked.

"Anything for you," Jackson replied, softly stroking her hand.

Jackson drove to the nearest McDonald's drive-thru and ordered a milkshake for Shantae. He asked if anybody wanted anything. Tianna wanted some fries and Tasha asked for a Big Mac. Darren didn't want anything. Jackson paid for the food and they drove off. Jackson took Tianna home first, and then Darren, and Shantae was last. Shantae thought she was spending the night with Jackson, but he had other plans.

Once Tianna got home, she went to her room and ate her fries. She took off her makeup, washed her face, and took a shower. She tied her hair up with a scarf and got into some comfortable clothes. She plopped down on her bed and began to watch TV. The whole time, she kept thinking about what Curtis had said after the basketball game. It was the first *real* conversation they'd ever had. Tianna didn't like the fact that Curtis was a bit egotistical and thought that he would be able to entice every girl he found cute or attractive.

She understood that she and Jackson were never going to be more than just friends.

She thought about what Tasha said about Jamal. She wanted a guy to look at her the same way she looked at Jackson. A guy that would give her the world. Could it be Jamal?

Maybe Jamal *did* have feelings for her?

Chapter Three

Tianna sure looked sexy tonight in that denim outfit. Those jeans hugged every symmetrical curve in her ass. Those perky breasts fit nice into that tank top. I wanted to grab them. She smelled and looked so good.

I can't believe I'm thinking these thoughts about my sister's best friend. All I could think was that I wished I hadn't brought Shantae along with me to the game. I would've preferred Tianna to be sitting up front in the car with me more than Shantae.

I also wonder what she and Curtis talked about. She seemed a little quiet and upset after meeting with him.

I swear if he hurts her, or does something to her, I will break him in two!

Jackson's reverie about Tianna ran wild in his mind as he drifted off to sleep.

The next morning Jackson awoke with Tianna still on his mind. He wondered if she would come to the house for dinner that night. He would talk to his sister and try to find out without revealing his interest in her best friend. He would ask his mother to cook Tianna's favorite dish, smothered grilled T-bone steak, and for dessert, strawberry with whipped cream cheese cake.

Man, would I love to eat one of those strawberries from her mouth, he thought.

Jackson climbed out of bed with a woody.

"Jackson!" Tasha said as she opened his bedroom door without knocking.

Jackson grabbed a pillow, placed it over his private part, and asked Tasha if she knew how to knock.

"Boy, I ain't gotta knock, and besides I done seen everything that you don't have," she teased.

"What do you want?"

"Mama said that we have guests coming tonight for dinner and that *you* need to be on your best behavior."

"Guests?"

"Yeah, a few members of the church are coming over."

"Aye, you inviting Tianna too?" Jackson wanted to know.

"Maybe or maybe not, why?"

"I just asked."

"You inviting Shantae to dinner?"

"Naww, she has to go take care of some important family business."

"Well, in that case, Tianna *is* coming to dinner," Tasha announced as she closed Jackson's bedroom door.

The news that Tianna was coming to dinner made Jackson's heart smile. He wanted to see and be near her and tonight was the perfect outing. He had to let his mother know what specifically to make for dinner, and wanted to know if she needed any help in the kitchen.

Jackson was a good cook, like his mother. He'd learned his culinary skills from watching her cook since he was five years old. Sharon welcomed her children into the kitchen whenever she made dinner. She wanted them to learn for themselves, and not depend on anyone to make them a home-cooked meal.

Jackson went to the restroom to relieve his bladder. He brushed and flossed his teeth, and gargled with Aim mouthwash. He checked his smooth chocolate skin and didn't find one pimple on his face. He licked his plumped lips and examined his hair. The waves were deep enough to make Michael Phelps seasick. Jackson picked up his boar brush to brush his hair, and applied coconut oil to make the waves shine.

He resembled an eighteen-year-old Morris Chestnut.

He took a shower and put on his gym shorts and wife beater to go shoot hoops with the guys.

Before he left home, Jackson saw his mother in the kitchen cooking breakfast. She warned him about being on his best behavior for the dinner guests. He requested Tianna's favorite foods and Sharon obliged.

He grabbed the keys to his Honda Accord off the table and drove to his first destination. He picked up his friend, Terrence, who everyone called "T.D." Then he went to pick up his friend Jeremiah. Finally, he picked up Andre. He drove over to his high school's outside basketball court, and they began to warm up. While they were warming up, instead of Jackson talking to his friends, he was silent because he was thinking about Tianna. *She looked so good last night.*

"Aye bro, you good?" Andre asked with a curious expression.

Jackson snapped out of his reverie.

"I'm cool, man."

"You sure? You've been quiet as if you're thinking about something."

Or someone, Jackson thought to himself.

"I'm good, bro."

"All right, let's play some ball, boi."

They played basketball until they got tired, or at least until Jackson was exhausted. After twenty minutes of play, he sat down and began thinking about Tianna some more. He hadn't really known that he had feelings for her until last night.

When Shantae called her a tar baby, he didn't like it. If Tianna was a tar baby, then he wanted her to be *his* tar baby. But he despised that derogatory name given to women with darker hued skin. In his mind, he *loved* dark skinned women. He loved all his Black women, with light or brown skin, they were Black women and that's all that mattered. But the darker girls seemed to go hand in hand with the sun. The sun made their skin glow like melted honey.

Tianna was intelligent and her personality was second to none. She carried herself well, and he saw the interior and exterior beauty. Shantae couldn't really compete with Tianna. No woman could. She had it *all*.

Jackson would be going away to college in the fall, so he didn't know if a relationship with Tianna was worth pursuing. He didn't want to cross the line since she was his sister's best friend who he had known for twelve years. She was like a *little* sister to him. Or that had been his thought process *before* he saw sexy Tianna last night. The tank top and jeans really got his attention.

Jackson dropped his homeboys off at home and stopped at a nearby convenience store to get gas. He walked into the store to pay for his gas when he accidently bumped into a girl standing next to another guy.

"Excuse me miss, my apologies," Jackson said as he looked directly into a familiar pair of eyes.

"Shantae!" Jackson said with trepidation and a look that said, "I thought you had some important family business, but you are in the store with another dude?"

Shantae could barely look Jackson in the eyes. She held her head down and placed her fingers between her bangs.

"Who are you?" The Lebron James look alike asked.

"Who are *you*? And why are you with my girl?"

"Your girl?"

"Yeah, Shantae is *my* girl."

"Shantae, is this true?"

She could hardly respond and continued with her head faced down and filled with embarrassment. She didn't answer, so Jackson answered for her.

"You know what? I'm done with yo ass. You can have him and anyone else you want!"

Jackson paid for his gas and drove off.

He pulled into his driveway ten minutes later, got out his car, and slammed the door.

He couldn't believe he let Shantae play him *again*.

Jackson was done with her and it couldn't have come at a better time. His interest in Tianna lessened the heartache of seeing Shantae with another guy. He hadn't been feeling her lately anyway, so her infidelity gave him reason to pursue Tianna without a guilty conscience.

Even though Jackson just found out he'd been cheated on, his interest in Tianna was at an all-time high. He didn't want her to be his rebound girl, though. Prom was coming soon, so he decided he would invite Tianna to be his date.

Jackson realized that the houseguests were coming over in two hours and he needed to get ready. He wanted to dress to impress. He was going to tell Tianna how he felt about her.

He put his shower on hold and went to the store so that he could get roses and a big poster board. He planned on asking Tianna to the prom, so he was going to write: "Will you go to prom with me?" on the poster board in big letters and give her the roses.

When Jackson arrived back home, he hid the roses and the poster board in his closet and went to take a shower. He wore his black T-shirt with his ripped jeans and his Jordan Retro shoes. He wanted to dress nice, but not to the point where people were questioning him.

He brushed his waves and applied his 100% coconut oil. He brushed and flossed his teeth to make sure his breath was fresh, and his pearly whites were shining. Finally, he put on his best smelling cologne. He was ready.

Sharon was in the kitchen cooking Tianna's favorite dinner and dessert. Jackson couldn't wait until *dinner* arrived.

The doorbell rang and Jackson rushed to answer it. He was so focused on Tianna he forgot that other houseguests were coming. He opened the door and it was Mrs. Johnson, the church lady who was always crying about her husband cheating on her and blaming his actions on the devil. She got on Jackson's last nerves.

"Hey, baby! Oooh, you smell nice and you looking *real* handsome. Who you looking cute for?" Mrs. Johnson asked as she gave Jackson a hug with her perfume and big breasts smothering his face.

"Nobody. I just want to look nice for the houseguests," Jackson replied.

Tasha came downstairs and started laughing once she saw Jackson. "Boy, you know you getting cute for somebody, don't be lying."

"Tasha, be quiet. I'm not trying to look all handsome for nobody."

"Both of y'all cut it out, we have a guest here and I need y'all to be on y'alls best behavior," Mrs. Norwood exclaimed.

A few minutes passed and the doorbell rang again. It was Mrs. Brown, the lady with the crying child. Thank God she didn't bring her little girl.

Jackson greeted Mrs. Brown and gave her a hug. Jackson was excited to see all the houseguests, but he was looking forward to seeing his future girlfriend, Tianna.

"Oooh Tianna just texted me," Tasha announced to everyone.

"Really? What did she say?" Jackson asked smiling and getting all excited.

Tasha gave Jackson a weird look. He was more excited than usual to hear Tianna's name.

"She said that she'll be here, but she's running late."

Jackson was bummed that Tianna was going to be late, but she was still coming and that's all that really mattered.

The doorbell kept ringing and three other guests came whom Jackson didn't know. Jackson was getting even more discouraged because he wanted to see Tianna.

The doorbell rang for the last time and Jackson walked over to the door expecting it to be another houseguest, but instead, it was Tianna.

"Hey, Tianna," Jackson said with a smile on his face.

"Hi, Jackson." Tianna smiled back.

Jackson felt his stomach fill with butterflies as he hugged her. She was looking sexy as ever. She had on a long sleeve black low-cut top, some dark skinny jeans, and red bottom heels. She had her hair in a high sleek bun, and wore big silver hoop earrings with a silver shiny heart necklace. Her low-cut top showed just enough cleavage to make

Jackson go wild. She smelled like strawberries and watermelon combined. Sweet. Jackson wanted to sniff her all night.

Tasha heard Tianna's voice and came rushing downstairs.

"Oooh girl, you look good! Now I see why you were late." Tianna blushed and thanked her for the compliment.

Sharon began cooking a little late, and dinner was going to be ready in ten minutes. The houseguests sat in the living room talking about random adult topics.

Tianna and Tasha were talking, and Tasha excused herself to go take a quick shower before dinner.

"You look beautiful, Tianna," Jackson said as he gave a nervous smile trying not to look at Tianna's cleavage.

"Aww thank you, Jackson. By the way, is Shantae coming for dinner?"

"Nah. I haven't told anyone yet, but she and I broke up earlier today."

"Really? What happened? Unless you don't want to talk about it," Tianna asked, acting like she wasn't happy that they were no longer together.

She felt bad for Jackson, but at the same time, she was happy because she never liked Shantae.

"Nah, it's fine. She lied and told me that she wasn't going to make it to dinner tonight because she had to take care of some 'important family business,' but I saw her today at the convenience store with another guy. When I went to confront her, she had nothing to say and looked guilty as hell. I told her it was over."

"I'm so sorry to hear that. You deserve better anyway. It's her loss."

"I guess," Jackson said in an uncertain tone.

"Who was the guy?"

"I have no idea. He looked like a watered down Lebron James. I have never seen him before."

"You could do a lot better. But are you okay?" Tianna asked with concern.

"Actually, I'm not really all that heartbroken."

"Really? Why not?"

"Because, there is something I have to tell you."

"What is it?"

When Jackson was about to ask Tianna the big question, they were interrupted.

"Tianna, I need your help upstairs!" Tasha yelled at the top of her lungs.

"I'm sorry for my children, they seem to have lost their manners tonight," Mrs. Norwood explained to the guests.

Tianna excused herself from Jackson to help her friend. She walked up the winding stairs and opened Tasha's bedroom door.

Jackson watched her walk with a silent smile plastered across his face. He shook his head side to side and pinched himself to make sure he wasn't dreaming.

How could Tasha's big mouth interrupt me when I was about to ask Tianna an important question? She could have waited a little longer. As a matter of fact, why couldn't whatever she needed wait? Why couldn't she do it herself? Jackson thought, irritated by his sister's abrupt interruption.

"Mom, do you need any help in the kitchen?" Jackson asked.

"No, I just need help understanding what has gotten into you and Tasha tonight. I told both of y'all to be on your best behavior. Instead y'all are yelling like some animals."

"Mom, Tasha was the only one yelling, not me."

Mrs. Norwood shook her head and walked to the kitchen to start getting the plates and silverware ready for dinner.

Tianna came out of Tasha's room to find Jackson standing outside listening to their conversation through the door. Tianna laughed and asked Jackson what he was doing.

"Umm, I was just looking for my glasses."

"You don't wear glasses, Jackson."

"Uhh, you're right. I guess I need to get my eyes examined," Jackson said as he got up from the floor and brushed off his hands and knees.

"So, what did you have to tell me earlier?"

"Oh yeah, I was gonna tell you that—"

"Dinner is ready, everyone!" Mrs. Norwood shouted to the guests downstairs.

"Damn it!" Jackson said out loud.

"Boy, don't use that language in this house! Now come and eat."

"Umm. You can just tell me later." Tianna smiled.

And she, Tasha, and Jackson walked into the main dining room. The room had Black American decor and a picture of the first Black president, Barack Obama, on the wall. There was a picture of Malcolm X and Dr. Martin Luther King Jr. The drapes were a satin red with gold tones. An elegant chandelier hung in the center of the fifteen-foot-long cherry hardwood dining table and chairs. The table could seat twelve guests comfortably.

Mrs. Norwood outdid herself. Spread neatly across the dining table was T-bone steak, salmon with lemon and lime, mashed potatoes, breaded baked macaroni and cheese, collard greens, corn on the cob, red beans, baked fries, cabbage, buttered rolls, hot-water cornbread, and romaine salad with cucumbers, tomatoes, boiled eggs and croutons. For dessert, there was chocolate cake, strawberry cheesecake, and banana pudding pie. Everything was served with water, tea, and lemonade.

"Sharon, Sharon, God bless your culinary skills. Everything looks delicious. You really know how to welcome guests in your home," Mrs. Brown announced.

"Why thank you, Mrs. Brown, and you are welcome at any time. Mi casa es su casa."

Everyone laughed because Mrs. Norwood was always trying to practice her Spanish skills.

"Please, please have a seat and dig in. Don't be shy," Mr. Norwood said as he entered the room. He was on an important business call when all the guests arrived. He explained his absence and apologized.

Tianna sat down and Tasha pulled out her seat to sit next to her, but Jackson was steadfast and sat in the seat right next to Tianna. He gestured for his sister to "shoo," and thanked her for pulling out *his* chair.

"Boy, I ain't pulled out no chair for you. You better get up. I'm sitting here."

"Tasha, go away. There are plenty of chairs, now go find one."

"Jackson Jeffrey Norwood, get your little behind up and let your sister sit there." When Mrs. Norwood said Jackson's full name, she and everyone knew that she meant business.

"Jackson, do what your mother asked," Mr. Norwood reiterated.

Jackson reluctantly got up from the seat, but not without a huff of annoyance. Tasha was messing up his *Mack* game. He wanted to sit next to Tianna, but since Mrs. Brown sat to the left of her, he had to sit farther away. He walked around to the other side of the table and sat directly in front of Tianna as he continued to stare into her eyes the entire time they ate.

Tianna was so nervous that she barely ate her food. She ate a salad topped with olive oil dressing.

"Why aren't you eating your favorite, T-bone steak?" asked Jackson.

"Yeah, you always eat my mother's steak," Tasha said.

Mrs. and Mr. Norwood, along with the other guests, awaited Tianna's response.

She had all eyes on her, as if Jackson staring her down the entire time wasn't enough to ruin her appetite. She sat there trying to think of a good excuse as to why she wasn't slobbering down that T-bone steak and licking the A.1. Steak Sauce from her petite fingers.

"I... I... umm, I had my mother's dinner before I arrived. You know how my mother is, she gets offended if you don't eat at least some of her home-cooked meals."

Tianna stuttered without looking up and kept nibbling at her salad with her salad fork. Everyone stared at Tianna, looking appalled. Even if Tianna had eaten her mom's food before she came, she always ate Mrs. Norwood's food. Especially her T-bone steak.

Throughout the meal, Tianna felt Jackson staring at her and she didn't say anything. Jackson was eating his steak while looking at her cleavage and lips. Tasha looked at Jackson staring at Tianna, and even though she wanted to call him out in front of the guests, she decided she was going to wait until later to ask why he had been acting so weird.

"Tianna, how has everything been lately?" Mrs. Norwood asked politely as she took a bite of her steak.

"Everything has been great."

"I heard that prom is coming up. Is there anyone in particular that you're going with? Or has anyone asked you out to the prom?"

Once Jackson heard the question, he sat up and stared Tianna down even more as he waited for her answer. He hoped nobody had asked her to prom because *he* wanted to take her.

"Well… this one guy asked me, but I don't really know him very well."

"Who asked you to prom?" Jackson quickly blurted out loud without even thinking.

"Um, you know Curtis?

"Yeah—ohh, is that why you went to talk to him after the basketball game?" Jackson asked.

"Yeah."

"All right, let's not question Ms. Tianna too much. Let her enjoy her meal," Mr. Norwood said as he poured lemonade into his glass.

Tianna was grateful when Mr. Norwood interrupted the conversation to get the spotlight off her and her prom date.

The whole dinner table was quiet for a good five minutes until Tasha asked Jackson who he was taking to the prom.

Jackson looked at Tianna. She looked at him and their eyes met and she took a sip of her water.

The room was so quiet that you could hear a pin drop.

"Why would you ask him such a thing? You know he's taking Shantae," Mr. Norwood announced, not knowing that Jackson and Shantae were no longer together.

Jackson hadn't let anyone know what Shantae did, and that he was single now.

"Ummm, Shantae and I are not together," Jackson said.

"Whatttttt?" Mr. and Mrs. Norwood said simultaneously.

"Aaahhh haaaaa! I told you that she was leaving you for Jamal," Tasha teased.

"Tasha, leave your brother alone," Mr. Norwood said.

"You and Shantae broke up? When?"

"That's okay, baby. You're a good-looking boy and you will find another girl," Mrs. Brown assured him.

Yes, Mama. We broke up today at the convenience store when I went to put gas in my car."

"What happened?"

"She lied and told me that she was taking care of family business, but she with another guy."

"Aww, are you feeling okay, baby?" Mrs. Brown asked.

"Yes ma'am. I'm fine. It was for the best."

"Wow, I'm surprised you're handling this so well, son."

"You're not heartbroken or anything?" Tasha chimed in.

"No, not really. I was losing interest in her."

"So, who do you plan on taking to prom?" his mother asked.

"I don't know yet," Jackson lied, knowing that he planned on asking Tianna to the prom. He didn't want to embarrass her in front of the guests. He also didn't want Tasha to know that he liked her. He knew that she would flip out.

"I can't wait for prom. If nobody asks me, I'm going with Tasha and Darren," Tianna announced, hoping that Jackson got the clue to ask her.

The table was filled with laughter and chatter as Mrs. Brown told a story to lighten the mood. Twenty minutes went by and Jackson still had not asked Tianna to prom. He wanted to get it over with before the night ended because he was nervous.

After dinner was over and the houseguests left, Jackson was upset with himself because he didn't have the confidence to ask Tianna to the prom.

Tianna asked Mr. and Mrs. Norwood if she could spend the night. They said that she was always welcome in their home, but to make sure she asked her mother.

Tianna confirmed it with her mother and let the Norwoods know that it was fine.

Jackson was so excited that she was spending the night at his house. He had the whole night and next morning to ask her to the prom.

It was nine p.m. and Tianna and Tasha were in Tasha's bedroom gossiping and talking about prom, makeup, and how they were going to do their hair.

"Do you want me to do your makeup and hair for prom? Cuz you know I will hook you up for free," Tasha said.

"I think I'll find a professional for my hair and makeup. No offense to you, Tash, but I want to do something different."

"I'm getting my hair straightened with curls. It's gotta be poppin!"

Tianna wished she wasn't so tender headed because she couldn't do many styles. She pondered what hairstyle wasn't going to hurt the most, and what would look cute on her.

"Hmm. I think I'm planning on slicking my hair into a high ponytail and getting a long straight drawstring ponytail, and attaching it to my hair.

"Oh, that'll be cute. But are you sure that's going to look right with your natural coils?" Tasha asked.

"You're right, I need to let my coils do what they do. They get angry when I try to oppress them." Tianna laughed.

"Are we talking about hair or slavery?" Tasha chuckled.

Tasha and Tianna were startled by a knock on the door.

"Yeah, who is it?" Tasha inquired.

"Can I come in? It's Jackson."

Tianna grabbed her blouse and buttoned it, and jumped up to take a quick once over in the mirror. She fumbled with her Afro puff and applied a quick coat of her strawberry luscious lip-gloss.

"Jackson, what do you want?"

"I need to ask Tianna a question."

"Go away. She doesn't have time for newly ditched rebound guys."

"Tasha, behave and let him in." Tianna curled her lips and batted her baby doll eyes.

Tasha couldn't resist that irresistible move that Tianna often did with her lips and dark beaded eyes to get her to behave.

Jackson opened Tasha's bedroom door and sat down on the bed right next to Tianna. Tianna felt her body flush, and if she weren't of a darker hue, she would have been red as an apple.

"What is that you are wearing, girl? You always smell good and be driving me insane."

"It's just the Japanese Cherry Blossom lotion from Bath and Body Works."

"You need to stock up on that scent."

"Jackson, what do you want?" Tasha said with annoyance.

"I'm here to ask Tianna a question. I've been waiting to ask her all night."

Tianna looked directly into Jackson's eyes and then briefly looked away. She couldn't hold her stare into his bedroom Tupac Shakur eyes. She looked down at her red bottom shoes as if there was gum stuck underneath them.

Tasha looked at her friend fidgeting, but didn't say anything. Instead, she rescued her by telling Jackson to get out. She pulled him off her bed, led him out the door, and locked it.

Tianna couldn't help but wonder what Jackson wanted to ask her. She wanted him to ask, but then again, she didn't. She didn't know what was about to come out of his mouth.

She wasn't in the mood for any surprises.

Chapter Four

Prom was two weeks away and Tianna still didn't have a date. Well, she'd been asked but declined Curtis's invitation. She didn't want to go to the prom with him. She viewed him asking her as some type of setup or game. Her declining his proposal made Jamal ecstatic. He couldn't believe Curtis, his *homeboy* went behind his back to ask *his* girl to the prom. She wasn't *his* girl, yet, but soon she would be. She was going to be his future wife and have a lot of his babies, Jamal imagined. But after he made it to the NBA. He had his present and future planned, but Tianna didn't know that Jamal's present and future included her.

The seventh period bell rang and students walked and talked in the busy hallway. They cast their votes for the King and Queen of Fox Tech High School. Jamal had the entire basketball and football teams cast their votes for him and Tianna.

Shantae had her girls, the cheer squad, and volleyball team, cast their votes for her and Jamal.

"Heyyyy, Jamal," Shantae said as she swished her full figure hips while sucking on a strawberry Blow Pop, walking within inches of his backside.

Jamal had no interest in Shantae, or any other girl for that matter, if it wasn't Tianna.

"What's up, Shantae? Jamal ask as he tilted his head in an upward motion.

"You." She giggled along with her friends Amber and Renee. "Do you have a date to the prom?" Shantae asked.

"Naw, not at this moment."

"Do you want to go together?" Shantae inquired, and before Jamal could answer, she blurted out, "I'll be ready by seven p.m. See you at my house." She swished away with her Blow Pop in her mouth and girls by her side.

Jamal shook his head side-to-side, searching for Tianna. They were supposed to walk home together and discuss an upcoming project due in physics class next week.

Jamal didn't have to search long because as soon as he closed his locker, Tianna was on the other side of it.

"Ohh, shit!" Jamal was startled.

"Watch yo mouth. You know you better not let yo mama JoAnn hear you swearing," Tianna joked.

"Naww, I won't. What's up with you creeping up on a brother like that?"

"My bad. I overheard Shantae ask you to the prom and for you to pick her up by seven p.m."

"Yeah, I'm taking her to the prom. So, who are you going to the prom with? Curtis?"

"Nope. He asked me but I declined. I have someone else in mind," Tianna admitted as she flashed her megawatt smile.

Jamal was not aware that the person she was referring to was Jackson.

Jamal and Jackson were acquaintances. They were not friends, meaning they felt indifferent about each other. The reason for their indifference was that Jackson always thought Jamal had a crush on his ex-girl Shantae. Jackson didn't like the way Jamal was always vying for Tianna's attention, or their tight-nit friendship. Jackson felt that Jamal was stealing both of his women.

He never confronted Jamal, but the looks Jackson gave him at basketball practice said plenty.

When they divided up into teams, Jamal and Jackson always played against each other. They were never joined at the hip like buddies even though they were on the same basketball team.

When Tianna and Jamal walked out the school doors heading home, Jackson was waiting at the edge of the stairway looking for Tianna.

When he saw them together, he mumbled under his breath with a huff. "What is this guy doing with my girl?"

Tianna wasn't his girl. But in Jackson's mind she was, if only she knew it.

"Hey, Jackson. What are you up to?" Tianna asked, curious to know why he wasn't in his car on his way home.

"I'm waiting to take you home," Jackson said.

"That's sweet of you, but I don't need a ride today. Jamal and I are headed to my house to work on our physics project," she explained.

Jackson looked at Jamal and smirked. He asked Jamal why he wasn't making plans to take his ex-girl to the prom. Jamal didn't know how Jackson knew about him taking Shantae to the prom since she'd only asked him fifteen minutes ago.

"I got plenty of time, so don't you worry about that, bro," Jamal said with irritation.

"I'm not. Remember, she's *my* leftovers. Add a few sprinkles of salt and she should be fine."

"Yeah, looks like you know *all* about salt, since you seem so salty about me taking her to the prom."

Jackson didn't care about Jamal taking Shantae to the prom. His salty attitude came because he was walking with Tianna, and they were headed to her house to work on an *alleged* project.

"No salt at all. Tianna, are you sure you don't want me to take you home?"

"If you are willing to give both of us a ride, I will take it."

"Sure, let's go. I don't have a problem with him," Jackson said with the straightest face he could muster up. He *did* have a problem with Jamal. A big problem.

Tianna and Jamal got into Jackson's car. Tianna sat in the front with Jackson while Jamal sat inches from Tianna in the backseat.

Jackson pulled out his iPhone to connect to his playlist. The sounds of Aaliyah's voice serenaded them through the speakers,

"Let me know. Let me know."

"What you know about this song?" Tianna asked Jackson.

"What you mean what do I know about this song?" Jackson smiled.

"It's one of my all-time favorite songs," Tianna said as she began singing along with Aaliyah. Jamal and Jackson were amazed by her beautiful voice. She sounded identical to Aaliyah. They were not only taken aback by Tianna's natural beauty, but she could sing, too! Whoever got her to be his girl would hit the jackpot.

Tianna continued to sing and leaned her head back on the headrest with thoughts of Jackson.

She thought about what it would be like to be his girl. She wanted to know.

She smiled at Jackson, not once but twice. He smiled back.

Jamal saw the unspoken body language between them and kneed Tianna's seat to break their trance.

"My bad. Ummm, did you get all the supplies needed for the project?" Jamal interrupted without a good reason to do so.

"Yes, Jamal, for the umpteenth time." She didn't want to end the moment she and Jackson were sharing. She was annoyed with Jamal but tried not to show it.

Jackson looked at Jamal through his rearview mirror as if to say, "cock blocker."

Jamal smirked at Jackson and couldn't wait to get out of his car. He didn't know why Tianna suggested that he ride with them. He could have walked and met her at her house. The more he thought about Jackson and Tianna's connection, the more insecure and hopeless he became about making Tianna his girl and future wife.

What is up with Jackson? And why is he acting like he's all into Tianna? I know his type. He only wants one thing from her. He could never give her what I could give her, and that's unconditional love. I could give her a future. A future with marriage and children. When I make it to the NBA, I could fulfill her dreams with reality. He pondered their future as he drifted off into a reverie.

Jackson, Jamal, and Tianna drove up to her home Tianna and Jamal got out the car. Her mother, Bernadette was outside watering the plants and lawn.

"Hi, Mrs. Thompson," Jackson sang with a smile.

"Hey, baby," she responded as she took a whiff of her Benson & Hedges cigarette while sucking her teeth.

"Good afternoon, Mrs. Thompson," Jamal said.

"Hey, Jamal. You know you boys can call me Bernadette. I'm not a grandma, yet. I'm still fine as wine," she said as she guided her hand down the left side of her hip.

"Mama, stop!" Tianna interrupted before her mother got too sexual and out of hand about her age and how fine she was. Bernadette loved acting like she was still in high school.

She didn't look her age, and she was only seventeen years older than Tianna. She looked more like Tianna's older sister. She loved when people complimented her on her youthful looks

She would bat her eyes with delight.

The neighborhood boys called her Mrs. Parker from the movie *Friday*, because of the outfits she wore when she watered the lawn. Her demeanor when she saw men walking down the street reeked of looseness.

"Tianna, hush yo mouth and go on inside to help your grandmother with her hair. She has an interview tomorrow at another library. Those people refuse to promote her after working for them for twenty years."

"Mama, Jamal and I need to work on our physics project. That's the reason he's here with me."

"Tianna, I'll see you at school tomorrow," Jackson said. "Bye, Mrs. Thompson—I mean, Ms. Bernadette," Jackson prepared to drive off. He didn't say anything to Jamal, acting as if he wasn't there.

"See you, and thank you for the ride." Tianna said.

"Bye, Jackson," Bernadette and Tianna said in unison.

Jamal stood there, wanting to flip Jackson off, but didn't want to do so in front of Tianna and Mrs. Thompson.

"Well, I guess you are going to have to start that project *after* you help your grandmother," Bernadette hissed.

"Jamal, do you mind if I help my grandmother before we start? You can just wait in my room for me."

"Nah, do what you got to do. I ain't going nowhere." Jamal chuckled. He knew Tianna was upset, but also wanted to take some time to get acclimated in her room. He didn't mind being there all by his lonesome self to take in her every scent and fantasize about their future together.

"Are you sure you don't mind?"

"I want Grams to look good for her interview, and I know you got the magic touch to make it happen," he said, rubbing his hands together like he was a magician. Jamal called Grandma Debby "Grams," short for grandma.

"Thanks," Tianna said as she hugged Jamal and kissed him on the cheek.

Just as Tianna hugged and kissed Jamal, she heard a familiar voice behind her.

"Tar Baby! What do you think you're doing?"

When she turned to see who was speaking to her, she looked directly into *those* eyes and had to refrain from slapping the smack out of her. Tianna had had it with her, and she despised that name, *Tar Baby*. Those eyes belonged to Shantae!

Shantae and her posse, Amber and Renee, stood within inches of Tianna and Jamal. Shantae only lived a few houses from Tianna, so it wasn't unusual for them to see each other more often than preferred.

"What do you think I'm doing? This ain't your business, Shantae."

"Jamal is my business. He's taking *me* to the prom." She hissed and rolled her eyes like she was having a seizure. When Shantae rolled her eyes, it wasn't cute. It was quite the opposite.

"So, what does him taking you to the prom have to do with me?"

"Not a damn thing, so keep your paws off him," Shantae barked.

"Wait a minute, Shantae. Let's get this straight. I'm only taking you to the prom. That means nothing more and nothing less. We are not in a relationship," Jamal said with a confused look on his face.

"I know, but I still don't want Tar Baby hugging and kissing all over you. Can you at least wait until after prom for all that?" she pleaded.

She tried her best to save face because she was embarrassed that Jamal put her in her place about their non-relationship status.

"Look, Shantae, no disrespect to you, but I'm actually not interested in taking you to the prom. You're *not* my girl."

That was it! Shantae had enough of her ego being shot out of space for the day and she lashed out at Jamal.

"You know what, Jamal? F*ck you and Tar Baby too!" She stomped away telling her posse Amber and Renee to follow.

"I know that fast heifer didn't say, "F*ck you" in front of me. Doesn't she have any respect for her elders?" Ms. Bernadette said as she told Shantae to get the hell away from her house, talking to her daughter like that and disrespecting her.

"Fast tail got some damn nerves in front of my house with that mess."

"Mama, come on, let's go inside," Tianna said, urging her mother and Jamal to leave before it became World War Three on Hudson Ave. Tianna knew that her mother didn't take any mess and she would slap Shantae into next week if she got the chance. She didn't want her mother going to jail because of a minor child, let alone a hoochie like Shantae.

Bernadette turned off the water and rolled up the hose and all three went inside to avoid confrontation.

Jamal went to Tianna's room to begin their physics project while Tianna went into the living room where her grandmother waited for her hair to be done.

Bernadette followed Tianna into the living room, but she stopped in the kitchen to get herself a beer. She needed something to relax her and calm her riled nerves.

"What were y'all out there fussing about?" Grandma Debby asked.

"That fast tail Shantae was out there showing her ass and I had to put her in her place before I catch a case."

"Mama, Shantae is just like that. She does it to get attention. She's lacking love from home, so she takes it out on everyone not in her circle. I'm accustomed to her calling me names," Tianna said with trepidation in her voice.

"I don't give a damn about her problems at home. It ain't got nothing to do with you. She better keep that mess from around here. This is *my* house and you are *my* daughter."

Tianna was shocked and amazed at how angry her mother was, but most importantly, how she had her back for once in her life. Her mother had never shown her any affection or indicated how much she cared for her. The incident really riled her, and Tianna was elated to see the love.

"Grandma, how do you want your hair?" Tianna asked, trying to change the subject from Shantae.

"You know, how you do that updo that you did the last time."

"I don't remember what updo I did, Granny." Tianna laughed at how her grandmother demonstrated with her hands. She looked as though she was putting on a motorcycle helmet.

"Mama, you want me to do it since Tianna has a physics project to work on?"

"No, not really. Because the last time you did my hair, I looked like a hot mess. I mean, a hot *old* lady mess."

"No, you didn't. You're always exaggerating." Bernadette laughed.

"Tianna, go ahead upstairs and finish your project. I'll do this *old* lady's hair," Bernadette joked. Tianna and her grandmother laughed.

"All right, Granny, let me know if you don't like your hair and I will come down and do the finishing touches, so you won't look like nobody's grandma."

"Enough, Tar Baby!" Bernadette warned.

"Mama, stop calling me that. I'm beautiful! A beautiful and brilliant tar baby!" Tianna announced as she patted her hair and raised her perfect arched eyebrows.

Tianna being put down about her skin color never let her confidence waver. She often told the haters that her melanin be poppin!

"Yes, you are beautiful and smart, just like your grandma!" Grandma Debby said as she stuck out her tongue in a meddling way to Bernadette.

Bernadette took a whiff of her cigarette and blew the intoxicating nicotine smoke toward Tianna and her mother.

"Keep those cancer sticks to yourself. Tianna, go on baby, work on your project, and see what Jamal's doing in your room."

"Thanks, Granny," Tianna said as she gave her grandma a kiss on her cheek.

She gave her mother a playful push on her head and ran upstairs.

Chapter Five

Tianna quietly entered her room without knocking. She opened the door and saw Jamal looking at her scrapbook filled with pictures of her when she was a baby. Jamal didn't hear or see Tianna enter the room because he was lying on the bed with his back toward the door.

She snuck up on him, poked his six-pack abs with her fingers and said, "Boo!"

Jamal jumped but smiled when he saw Tianna's face. He looked like a kid in a candy store when he saw her. A kid on Christmas day opening his gifts.

"Hey, beautiful."

"Heyyy, Jammmal. Why you *always* call me beautiful?"

"Because you are, and it's what I see when I look at you."

"Jamal, stop. You are making me blush."

"I'm serious," he said, looking directly into her eyes.

Tianna twirled her hair and batted her beaded dark perfect eyes. Jamal loved when she did that. She usually did it when she was nervous or excited. She pursed her lips.

Jamal noticed everything about Tianna, but not only her exterior, he also admired her intelligence and the way she carried herself.

Tianna was pure and innocent. She didn't get caught up in gossip or want to be like any other hoodrat around the way or at school. She had her own unique style and demeanor. She was wife material, not a wifey. A wifey meaning, a baby mama without a ring. Tianna deserved the title of Mrs. Jamal Johnson.

Tianna and Jamal sat on her bed looking directly into each other's eyes in silence.

Their reverie lasted more than three minutes, as if they were reading each other's thoughts.

There was a knock at the front door. When Bernadette answered, she saw Jackson at the door holding a book.

"Oh, hi again, Ms. Bernadette. Tianna left her book in my car. Is it okay if I go up to her room and give it to her?"

"Sure, baby," Bernadette said as she stepped aside to let Jackson enter the house.

"Thanks."

"Hi, Mrs. Thompson," Jackson said to Grandma Debby as he skipped up the stairs to Tianna's room.

Jackson turned to the left when he got upstairs, the direction of Tianna's room. He saw her cute little bedazzling shiny name tag purse display that hung on the outside of her bedroom door.

He touched it and smiled in awe of how cute it looked.

He quietly opened the door without knocking and that's when he saw Jamal Johnson's lips kissing his girl. He slowly closed Tianna's bedroom door without a sound, ran downstairs, and out the front door without saying a word to Bernadette or Mrs. Debby.

He got into his car and drove off.

"Umm, what are we doing, Jamal?"

"Kissing."

"I know that, but *why* are we kissing?" Tianna asked. She waited for an answer, but he ignored her, and kept kissing her juicy lips.

"Tianna, did you get your—"

Bernadette opened the bedroom door and saw what Jackson had seen a few minutes before when he ran out the house.

Tianna and Jamal jumped at Bernadette's voice.

"Uhhh, you came to work on your physics project? Well, that don't look like no goddamn working on a project to me!"

"Mama, can you knock before entering?" Tianna asked.

"Girl, let me tell you something. This is *my* house. When you get your own place, then you can make those rules. In my house, I don't need to knock."

"But Mama…"

"But Mama, *nothing*. Did you get your book from Jackson?"

"No ma'am, what book?"

"He just left here and said that he had your book. He ran out my house like a fool, and I was wondering if you got your book from him?"

"What? Mama, Jackson was here just now?"

"Yes, he sure was and he ran out my house without saying a word," Bernadette said as she closed the door to leave the room.

Jackson must have seen her and Jamal kissing.

Oh no! Jackson saw me kissing Jamal? Or did he? How can I explain to him that he's the one I'm interested in, not Jamal? This was a mistake. A huge mistake. Jamal and I are just friends. I have to let him know that I have no interest in Jamal. He's the one I'm interested in.

"Jamal, can we continue this project tomorrow?"

"Yeah, but what's wrong?"

"Nothing. I have to go."

"Go where?" Jamal inquired.

Tianna searched for the right words to say without hurting Jamal's feelings, but she wanted her privacy so that she could call Tasha and ask about Jackson. She twirled her hair and blinked her eyes searching for tactful words to say.

"I have to….go finish my Granny's hair."

Jamal picked up on Tianna's body language and knew that she wanted him to leave. It hurt him deeply because he wanted to stay. Stay forever.

"All right, beautiful. I'll see you at school in the morning," he said. He tried to give her another kiss, but this time she didn't oblige. She moved her face and Jamal's kiss landed on top of her forehead.

He didn't quite understand her resistance toward him when they were just locking lips five minutes ago, but he knew that it had something to do with *Jackson Norwood.*

Dear Diary

It's been awhile since I have written. I apologize, but I have been so busy with school and prom is near. I have so much going on with Jackson and Jamal. Jackson, I adore, and I would love to be his girl. But Jamal, whom I've always loved as a friend, is showing interest in being more than friends.

Jamal and I kissed for the first time. He's the first boy that I've ever kissed, and it was special. He smelled so good and I didn't want to stop.

I have never thought of Jamal as a love interest, but what happened between us today was shocking and nice. I'm confused. I don't know how or what I'm feeling right now.

The kiss has stirred up emotions that I never knew I had for him.

Mama said Jackson came up to my room to bring me a book that I left in his car. She said he dashed out the front door without saying a word.

Did he see Jamal and I kissing? Oh my God, how could I explain it?

Tianna's iPhone beeped and she saw a text message from Jamal. She smiled as she read it.

Jamal: I had a great time today, beautiful.

Jamal: I hope I didn't do anything that would jeopardize our friendship. Let's get together again tomorrow to start *and* finish the project?

Tianna: Hey Jamal, we didn't do anything that I didn't want to do. I thought it was nice and I wouldn't mind doing it again.

She wrote this, but didn't push send. Instead, she deleted it and wrote:

Tianna: That would be fine and why don't we meet at the library?

Tianna suggested the library because she didn't trust Jamal or herself being alone together in her room.

She waited for him to respond, but there was only silence.

Her iPhone beeped with another text message, but it was from Tasha.

Tasha: Hey T, wyd? (what you doing?)

Tianna: I was texting Jamal about meeting after school tomorrow to finish our physics project. Wyd?

Tasha: I told U that U secretly feeling Jamal!! Lol. I wanna know if U want to go to the mall to look for prom dresses?

Tianna: Let's do it on Friday?

Tianna: Bet?

Tasha: Great, see U tomorrow.

Tianna was about to respond when she finally received a text from Jamal.

Jamal: Sorry, my phone battery died. The library is cool. Meet you after class.

Jamal: Goodnight, Beautiful. Jamal ended his message with a smiley face and a red heart emoji.

Tianna: Goodnight.

Chapter Six

The sound of the alarm awakened Tianna from her reverie. She pressed the snooze button. She wasn't asleep. In fact, she hadn't slept all night. She had so many thoughts and emotions running through her mind that sleep eluded her. She had an hour to take a shower, get dressed, eat breakfast, and wait for Tasha and Jackson to pick her up for school.

Her stomach was in knots. She didn't want to see Jackson because of what happened yesterday. She didn't know if he'd actually seen her and Jamal kissing. She didn't know what to say or whether to mention it.

Jackson had shown no interest in her, and what happened between her and Jamal *just happened*. It didn't mean anything. Or did it? She was so confused.

If it didn't mean anything, then why had she been up thinking about Jamal and the scent of his strawberry breath? Why did she want to taste the rainbow, *again*?

The alarms buzzed to make sure she was awake. Tianna pushed the snooze button and just lay there, deep in thought. She felt nauseated and really didn't want to go to school to face Jackson or Jamal. She took a deep breath and kicked the covers off her body to get out of bed. She placed her feet inside her comfortable SpongeBob SquarePants slippers. She'd had the slippers for years and they were three sizes too small. Her heels hung out the back and rubbed against the floor. Her mother tried once to throw them in the trash but Tianna found them and took them out. She called them her good luck charms. She swore that they kept monsters from hiding under her bed. Tianna was a little too old to believe in monsters, but her deadbeat father scared the living daylights out of her when she was three years old and she never got over it. She slept with a night light until last year, and recently she'd turned the switch off. But giving up her SpongeBob slippers was asking too much of her too soon. She wasn't ready.

"Tianna!" Bernadette yelled from downstairs.

Tianna couldn't hear because she was in the shower singing into her make believe microphone, the shower head.

She sang Beyoncé's "Irreplaceable."

She heard the bathroom door open, but she couldn't see because of the fog, and the music coming from the radio was a distraction. She grabbed the shower curtain and wrapped it around her like a towel.

"Tianna!"

"Yes, Mama."

"Can you pick up my clothes from the cleaners after school? I'll put the money on your dresser."

"Okay. No problem. But next time, can you knock?" Tianna asked.

"No, because this is my house!"

"But Mama, I still need my privacy. I'm growing up, ya know?"

"I don't care. I gave birth to you and I've seen everything you got." Bernadette laughed as she closed the door to leave for work.

Tianna rolled her eyes so that her mother couldn't see, turned off the water, and stepped out of the shower onto the floor mat. She immediately covered herself with a bath towel as soon as she heard the door open again.

"Oh and one more thing," Bernadette added unexpectedly. "Your dad wants to see you this weekend. He's buying you your prom dress. You better milk all the money you can out of his no-good ass."

"Yesssss, Mama," Tianna said so that her mother would leave and give her privacy.

She didn't feel comfortable around her father since he was never really a *father*. He only recently started claiming that she was his daughter, and since he'd been absent from her life before that, asking him for money was like begging a stranger.

Tianna got dressed, fixed her hair, and headed downstairs to eat a bowl of cereal. She only had twenty minutes until Tasha and Jackson arrived.

She sat at the table and turned on the TV to watch the latest local weather.

"Thunderstorms are expected at around one p.m. Take a light jacket because a cool wind chill is expected with the rain," the weatherman announced.

Texas weather was so unpredictable.

Tianna looked into the cabinet to get a bowl and reached for her favorite cereal, Lucky Charms with marshmallows. She poured the cereal into the bowl and walked to the refrigerator to get the 2% Borden's milk. She got a spoon from the drawer and sat down at the table to begin eating. She heard a car horn. She looked out the window and saw Jackson's car. She heard Tasha calling her name.

Tianna looked at the clock and thought to herself, *Why is he here ten minutes early? He's usually on time or late.*

She looked at Jackson from the window and he didn't even look at the house. He stared straight ahead and kept honking like they were late for school.

"I'm coming!" Tianna yelled out the window.

She didn't get to finish her breakfast. She grabbed an apple from the fruit bowl and rinsed it with cold water. She turned off the TV and set the security alarm.

She walked down the driveway and saw Shantae and her posse, Amber and Renee.

"Excuse me," Tianna said as she stumbled and almost stepped on Shantae's red bottom shoes.

"Can you watch where you're going, Blackie?" Shantae mumbled under her breath.

It was loud enough for Tasha to hear.

"Blackie? You better raise up out of here, Shantae, before you start something you can't finish!" Tasha had never liked Shantae, even when she was dating her brother, so she waited for the perfect time to set her straight.

"Whatever. I ain't got time for y'all tar babies," Shantae said as she sucked her teeth, but kept walking to catch the school bus.

"That's why yo ass is on the bus and not in the car." Tasha laughed as she opened the car door for Tianna.

Tianna got inside the car and greeted Tasha and Jackson, but only Tasha greeted her back with a "good morning." Jackson pretended like he didn't hear her, and as if she was invisible.

Tianna let out a sigh. Jackson looked through his rearview mirror at her and then stared out the window before he drove off.

He pushed play on his iPhone to start his early morning playlist. Jackson was young, but he had an old soul for old school music.

"Woo, I'm craving your body..."

Jackson sang along with Earth, Wind, and Fire while biting his bottom lip. Tianna loved when he bit his bottom lip. He looked so sexy. He glanced at Tianna in the backseat and they caught each other's stares. She quickly looked down and smiled. Jackson smiled inside at the sight of her beauty. He was in awe of Tianna, but he still couldn't get the picture of her kissing Jamal out of his head. He stayed up throughout the night thinking of Tianna and Jamal. He couldn't study for his economics exam because he was thinking about them.

"The reasons…," Jackson sang, trying to escape the vision of them.

"Who sings this song?" Tasha asked.

"Earth, Wind, and Fire," Jackson announced.

"Yeah? Well, let them sing it."

"Antt", Jackson made a noise that sounded like "ant" and placed his hand in front of Tasha's face as if to say, "talk to the hand."

She pushed his hand away.

"You better keep both hands on the wheel, you know you done had two accidents already. You get another one, DMV is taking your license and Dad is taking yo car," Tasha warned.

"That was years ago. Besides, one of the accidents is coming off my record soon. So you got to get yo own car, Big Head."

Jackson pulled into the school parking lot and Aaliyah's song, "Let Me Know" started to play. Jackson looked at Tianna and she reciprocated.

He knew that it was *her* song. They held each other's stares for what seemed like five minutes, but it was more like five seconds before he turned the car off and the music stopped. He waited until she got out of the car to give her a full body look over and clicked the remote to lock his car.

Tasha and Tianna had their first class together, so they walked a different way than Jackson.

"So, what's up with you and my brother?" Tasha inquired.

"Nothing, why you ask?"

"I saw him looking at you through that rearview mirror and I saw yo ass looking at him. I know you ain't feeling my brother. Are you?"

"Girll, nooooo. Ewwww, Jackson is like an older brother to me," Tianna lied.

"I'm just saying because you know how he gets down. And I don't want you to get your heart broken," Tasha said with concern. "And besides, I can't have my bestie with my brother. That wouldn't be cool."

"I know. But anyway, you're tripping. Jackson is like an older brother to me."

Tianna and Tasha arrived at their first class and sat in their assigned seats. Tianna couldn't help but think about Jackson and what Tasha said.

I wouldn't get involved with Jackson because I know he doesn't know how to be loyal. Loyalty is not in his DNA. The only girl he has ever been faithful to was Shantae. He was faithful, but she wasn't. I've seen him since the break-up, but I haven't seen him with another girl. According to Tasha, he's still the same playa, Tianna thought with uncertainty.

"Hey, what's up, beautiful?"

Tianna would know that voice anywhere. She turned, and Jamal stood over six feet, two inches right next to her. He smelled so delicious and looked fresh with his basketball shorts and letterman t-shirt.

What is he doing in my class? He's supposed to be at practice, Tianna thought to herself.

"Are we still meeting after school today?"

"Yes, but I have to stop at the cleaners and pick up my mother's clothes."

"All right, that's cool. I can go with you. I'll meet you in the hallway in our usual spot. See you later," Jamal said as he walked out of Tianna's first period class on his way to basketball practice.

"Girl, I told you about Jamal. That boy is in love with you," Tasha teased.

"No, he ain't. We are just good friends."

"Mmhmm, y'all gone be friends with them benefits," Tasha said as she gyrated her hips in a sexual manner.

"You so nasty. Stop being nasty. Stop being nasty!" Tianna said in her Mr. Brown dialect from the TV series, *Meet the Browns,* as she clapped her hands.

They both giggled as Mr. Washington walked into class to begin his lecture.

"All right guys, we are going to divide into two teams. Jamal and Jackson, y'all are going to be the captains," Coach Wilson announced.

Coach Wilson always chose Jackson and Jamal because they were the two best players on the team. Jamal and Jackson were both NBA prospects. Jamal played the point guard and Jackson was a shooting guard.

Jamal averaged twenty-six points per game, ten assists, and three rebounds. He was a good defender and shot fifty-five percent from the three-point line.

Jackson averaged twenty points, five assists, and eight rebounds per game. His field goal percentage was not as good as Jamal's, but it was still reputable.

"Guys, we got visitors attending next week's game. We not only have college scouts, but we have professional scouts from the San Antonio Spurs and the Dallas Mavericks. We have a scout flying in from the Los Angeles Lakers as well. You need to play the game of your life," Coach Wilson reiterated for the hundredth time this week. He often repeated himself to either make sure the guys understood, or he couldn't remember what he had already said. His memory wasn't the sharpest.

Curtis often mimicked the coach when he gave speeches. It was always the same speech in the exact same order that he had been saying since his older brother Calvin graduated from Fox Tech High School in 1997. Coach Wilson hadn't changed.

"One day, you're going to be husbands and fathers, and my desire is to teach you not only basketball skills, but the qualities and character of great men…"

Curtis stood behind the coach, mimicking while making all the same gestures he made. The guys laughed and Coach Wilson asked, "What's so goddamn funny?" As soon as he said that, Curtis stopped and got a serious look on his face as if he wasn't doing anything.

After the coach's speech, Jamal and Jackson chose their teammates.

But not until a coin was flipped to see who was choosing first.

Jamal won the coin flip and chose his boy, Curtis.

Curtis was a mediocre player, but he was Jamal's boy and a good defender and rebounder. He'd get upset if he wasn't on Jamal's team, or Jamal's number one player.

Jackson never chose Curtis so it was no big deal that Jamal chose him.

He was still pissed off about Jamal and Tianna. He wanted to punch him dead in his mouth as soon as he saw him in the gym, but he didn't want to get kicked off the team or suspended.

While guarding Jamal, Jackson kept reaching for the ball and accidentally slapped Jamal's wrist.

"Man, what's up?" Jamal barked.

"Dude, what's up with you?" Jackson returned his venom as he gave Jamal a push in his chest.

The coach blew the whistle and warned Jamal and Jackson of an early shower if they didn't want to play ball that morning.

Jamal threw the ball and hit Jackson in the chest with it.

"You mother fucker," Jackson said as he took a swing at Jamal, but missed because Jamal saw it coming and dodged his fist. Jamal punched Jackson with a right hook and then a left.

Jackson swung and hit Jamal right smack in the middle of his stomach and placed him in a headlock before punching him in his face.

Coach Wilson blew the whistle while the entire team ran to break up the fight.

"I'll teach you how to kiss *my* girl," Jackson said while being separated from Jamal.

"I didn't kiss Shantae."

"I'm not talking about Shantae! I don't care about her!"

"That's enough!" Coach yelled. "Hit the showers, NOW! If I see another punch, both of you are suspended and kicked off the team!"

Both players were essential to the Fox Tech basketball team and the season would be lost if either was suspended or kicked off the team. Even though the coach was upset and threatened to kick them off, he really didn't mean it. The most that would happen was a suspension. But Jamal and Jackson didn't know it.

Chapter Seven

The sounds of thunder could be heard vibrating off the school's walls. The lights kept flickering but didn't go off because they were run by a generator. The wind was strong and you could see notebook papers flying and swirling outside like a whirlwind. Students rushed in between classes trying to get to covered areas to shield them from the rain.

Tianna waited in the hallway at Jamal's locker. She didn't see him. Instead, she received a text message from him telling her to meet him out back by the covered parking lot.

She texted back, saying that she was on her way as soon as she got her umbrella from her locker.

Tianna walked to her locker to retrieve her umbrella. When she closed her locker, she saw Jackson at the end of the hallway looking in her direction.

She didn't know whether to wave or ignore him. She didn't know why he wasn't talking to her or what she had done to upset him. He had been acting strange since the day he dropped her and Jamal off at her house. Did he see Jamal and her kissing?

She decided to ignore him and walked the other way to avoid him.

She heard someone call her name.

"Tianna!" She turned to see Jackson waving to her.

She stopped and decided to wait for him.

He jogged to get to her as fast as he could. But as he got closer, she noticed his bruised face.

She had a look of concern and asked what happened.

He didn't want to talk about it. He asked if she wanted a ride home because he didn't want her walking or catching the bus in this weather.

She ignored him and asked, "What happened to your face, Jackson?" She touched him gently, examining his bruises.

"Do you need a ride home?" he repeated.

"Are you going to tell me what happened to you?"

"No, why would you care?"

"Well, if you are not going to tell me then I don't need a ride home," she said stubbornly as she turned to walk off. It was clear that she was concerned about Jackson and upset because he wouldn't tell her what happened.

He walked after her and grabbed her left hand, insisting that he was taking her home to make sure she got home safe.

She snatched her hand back and told him, "No, if you're not going to tell me what happened to your face."

Jackson grabbed her hand, pushed her against the wall, and looked her directly in the eyes. He told her that he was not taking "*no*" for an answer. She could leave with him willingly, or he would carry her, but it was *her* decision.

Her phone beeped with a text message from Jamal asking about her whereabouts.

Jackson looked at her phone to see Jamal's name.

"So, that's who you want to be with? Huh, Tianna?"

"Jackson, what are you talking about?" she asked as she continued to touch his wounds. He let her examine them.

He took her hands within his hands and gently kissed them.

"Jackson…" Tianna said before he leaned her against the lockers and began softly kissing her bottom lip. She closed her eyes in a state of shock, but didn't object to his tender soft lips. It smelled as though he had been chewing juicy fruit chewing gum. She could taste all the flavors and it tasted *good*. He began kissing her top *and* bottom lip. It was the most amazing feeling in the world. She didn't want it to end.

Jackson and Tianna were deep in their kiss when Tasha turned the corner and saw her brother and her best friend lip locking.

She couldn't believe her eyes. She didn't know whether to confront them, or cut off her friendship with her best friend of twelve years.

Tianna's phone beeped again; it was Jamal. The distraction of the phone halted their passionate kiss. She had to answer his message.

She looked down at her phone, and then searched Jackson's eyes for sincerity. He searched her soul for clarity. She was the one, he confirmed.

"Did I just see what I thought I saw?" Tasha asked, walking toward Jackson and Tianna.

Tianna turned to see a look of hurt, anguish, and disappointment on her friend's face.

She didn't know what to say, so she said nothing. She stood there with her head down reading Jamal's text messages.

"I can't believe you, Tianna! *You and my brother?*" Tasha asked in disbelief.

"Yo, Tash, it isn't her fault, it's mine. I'm in love with Tianna and you were going to find out sooner or later."

"In love with her? Jackson, you ain't no damn good. How could you be in love? Do you even know what love is?"

Tianna thought to herself, *did he just say that he was in love with me? What? This is all so confusing. I gotta go.* And instead of saying something, Tianna took off running out the back door toward the parking lot. She didn't even open her umbrella to shield the rain.

"See what you've done?" Jackson said to Tasha, and took off running after Tianna.

"Tianna! Tianna! Stop!"

As Jackson ran after Tianna, he bumped into Jamal, who had just seen Tianna run out the back door.

"Man, what the hell did you do to her?" Jamal demanded to know.

"Stay out of this, Jamal. This has nothing to do with you," Jackson said, continuing to call out to Tianna.

Tianna kept running in the pouring rain and thunderstorms. She didn't know what she was running from, but she ran to try and figure it all out. Jamal and Jackson were behind her in hot pursuit.

Tianna glanced back to see both guys running after her. She ran faster. She proceeded to run into traffic, and just as she ran toward Soledad and Commerce Street, she ducked into the Frost National Bank tunnel. Jamal and Jackson lost track of her as they continued to call her name.

Tianna was soaked and wet with rain and tears pouring down her face. She cried and cried while clenching and holding her stomach.

What had she done? She was in emotional turmoil. She had Jackson saying that he was in love with her. She had her best friend mad at her, and she had Jamal's passionate kiss.

What was she going to do? She was a mess and didn't want anyone to see her that way. And she still had her mother's dry cleaning to pick up.

Tianna peeped around the corner to see if Jackson and Jamal were still in sight. She didn't see them.

She took out her compact powder make-up mirror and examined her face. "*Ewwww,*" she thought to herself.

Tianna took out a trial size pack of Kleenex, blew her nose, and wiped her tears. She retrieved her bubble gum flavored Victoria's Secret lip balm and puts it on her lips.

She gave herself a once over, closed her compact powder, and placed it back in her purse.

The weather couldn't be any worse and it didn't seem like it was stopping anytime soon.

Tianna opened her umbrella and proceeded to walk to the dry cleaners to pick up her mother's clothes.

As soon as she opened the door to Melvin's Cleaners and closed her umbrella, she looked into Jamal's bruised face. She covered her mouth in disbelief and her lips started to tremble.

"Jamal, what are you doing here and what happened to your face?"

Jamal didn't speak; he couldn't, not at that moment. He took her in his arms and hugged her so tight. She let him embrace her and needed to feel his comfort. He held her and didn't want to let go.

He finally spoke, "Beautiful, don't ever leave me like that. Do you know what it would do to me if something were to happen to you?" He continued to hold her in a tight, genuine hug.

"I love you, Tianna!" he whispered in her ear. "I love you," he repeated as tears poured down Tianna's face. Hearing those words, not once, but twice today from the two men that she admired the most was emotionally overwhelming.

What was she going to do? Tianna didn't want to hurt anyone. She loved both Jackson and Jamal. She loved her friend, Tasha. But somebody was going to get hurt. So Tianna continued to cry in Jamal's arms while he confessed his love for her.

"I've loved you all my life, from the day I saw you in first grade. I want to marry you and make you my wife." He whispered all the right words in her ear and she believed him. Jamal's character was that of a good guy. He was never a "thot chaser" like Jackson used to be before he got with Shantae. In fact, she had never known Jamal to have a girlfriend.

Jamal finally released Tianna from his embrace, looked her directly in her eyes, and whispered to her, "I want you to be mine, Tianna. I want you to be my girl. Not right now only, but for life." He wiped and kissed the tears that continued to flow down her face.

"I know this is a lot for you to think about, and it's been one of those days, but I want you to be mine."

Tianna couldn't answer. All she could do was cry and mumble, "What happened to your face?"

"It's nothing and I'm fine. Don't worry about it. I gotta get you home."

He was more concerned about her than his bruised face. She looked down at his hands and saw scars there as well. She held on tight to his hands and rubbed her fingers over his wounds. Tianna didn't connect Jamal and Jackson's wounds to each other. All she knew was that both of them had bruises, fresh wounds.

Tianna paid for her mother's dry cleaning and she and Jamal caught the bus to her house.

Chapter Eight

The rain finally ceased when Tianna and Jamal got off the bus to walk to Tianna's house. As they turned the corner, they saw Jackson's car sitting out front. Jackson sat in the car, but got out when he saw Tianna and Jamal walking toward the house.

Jamal couldn't believe why Jackson wouldn't go away and wondered why he was in front of the house. Tianna had the same thoughts that Jamal had. She wondered why he wasn't at work.

Jackson walked up to Tianna and Jamal and tried to take Bernadette's dry-cleaning clothes from Jamal and told him that he could take it from here.

Jamal refused to give Jackson the clothes and told him that he had it and he didn't need his help. He'd had enough of Jackson for one day and he wanted to continue beating his ass, but restrained himself because he respected Tianna and her home.

He wouldn't dare punch Jackson in front of Tianna or her mother's home.

"Jackson, what are you doing here?" Tianna asked.

"I came to check on you."

"I'm fine. I appreciate your concern but I'm a big girl and I can take care of myself."

Jackson didn't hear a word she said. He was too busy staring Jamal down and wanting him to leave. He practically burned a hole through him, and if he said anything out of line, he was going to finish the fight this time.

"Tianna, I *need* to talk to you. It's urgent," Jackson explained.

Tianna turned to Jamal and said, "Jamal, please go inside and wait for me in my room. Please." Tianna emphasized, *please* as she gave him the door key.

Her grandmother should be home by now so she didn't give him the security code for the alarm system.

Jamal took the key and whispered to Tianna that he would be inside if she needed him. Tianna gave him a look to say that she would be fine and he was not needed at this time.

Jackson stood there with his hands in his pockets, irritated because he wanted Jamal gone and far away from Tianna.

Jackson asked if she would take a ride with him and she obliged.

Jackson opened the car door for Tianna to enter. This was the *first* time he had ever opened her car door. She was elated and a little bewildered.

Jamal stared out of Tianna's bedroom window and watched her and Jackson leave.

He pondered what Jackson was up to and fantasized about breaking his neck if something were to happen to her.

"Are you going to tell me what happened to your face?" Tianna asked.

"I thought your boy would have told you by now."

"Who, Jamal?"

"Pstttt, yeah, him." Jackson didn't say his name and really didn't want to talk about *him*.

Jackson told her what happened between him and Jamal in gym class and how it started. But he left out a pertinent fact, that *he* started the fight because he saw Jamal kissing her in her room the other day.

Tianna couldn't believe her ears. Not only about the fight, but the reason they fought. It was because of *her*. She didn't want them fighting, but she felt special knowing that they were fighting over *her*. She had to shake that thought and tell him how much she disapproved of their actions, and that they could have been kicked off the basketball team, and how it could be detrimental to their basketball careers.

She touched his bruises as he held one hand on the steering wheel while holding her hand that touched his bruises. He began to kiss her hand. She flinched at first, but let him continue. They pulled into the parking lot of Plez Park. Jackson killed the car engine and plugged his iPhone into his charger and changed the radio tuner to Bluetooth to play his playlist.

Tianna's song began to play, and as soon as she began to sing, Jackson changed it.

"I know you didn't," she said. "How are you going to do me like that, Jackson?"

He smiled with his pearly white teeth showing.

"Oh, that's your song, huh?" he said, and then pushed play on his iPhone and her song started playing where it left off.

Let me know…….

Jackson did the little thing he did with his bottom lip and then leaned in to kiss Tianna. She closed her eyes and leaned into him too. Their teenage tongues started dancing to the sounds of Aaliyah. Jackson placed his right hand on Tianna's left breast and she moved his hand. He placed his left hand on her right breast as if that was going to make a difference. Tianna removed his left hand and held both of his hands tight on top of her lap, letting him know not to take it to *that* level. She wasn't ready. He obliged and didn't do anything she didn't want to do. He was a gentleman and respected her wishes. They continued to kiss and didn't appear to be coming up for air anytime soon. It felt natural to them. Besides, how could she look into his eyes after slobbing him down? The only thing that pushed them apart was the sound of Tianna's phone beeping with a text message.

Jamal: Yo, where you at, beautiful?

Jackson let out a breath of exhaustion. He was *tired* of Jamal. He wanted to spend time with Tianna, not only to ask her to be his girl, but to ask her to the prom. He couldn't do either with Jamal constantly texting her.

"Can you please turn off your phone?"

"Jackson, I can't. My mother could be trying to contact me. I think I better be getting back home."

"Why? We just got here," he tried to explain.

"I know but I have to work on my project and I don't want to leave Jamal at my house alone for too long."

"Jamal, that's right. You can't keep *him* waiting for long."

"Why you say it like that?"

"Like what?"

"Like that." She repeated how he said it.

The way she mimicked him made Jackson laugh and before she knew it, they were laughing and mocking each other.

The look in her eyes turned serious, as she hadn't forgotten about the fight between Jackson and Jamal. She looked at his bruises and asked him to promise her that he would avoid any confrontation with Jamal. He reluctantly promised her that their "mini beef" was over.

She kissed him one last time on his cheek and his smile made her heart flutter. She really, really liked Jackson. She wanted to call it love, but didn't know if it was too soon to declare such a strong word. She also thought about her friend Tasha and how she would never approve of a relationship between her and her brother. Her heart broke at the thought of losing Jackson or Tasha. She never wanted to lose either of them. But having both was impossible. The thought of choosing between Jackson and Tasha turned her blue sky gray.

Jackson started the car and they headed to Tianna's house. The ride was quiet and full of crazy thoughts running through their minds.

Jackson wanted Tianna and Tianna wanted Jackson, but too many people would not approve of them being together. Neither Tasha nor Jamal would approve. She would lose both of her friends. Was Jackson worth it?

They pulled up at Tianna's house.

"You black b*tch!" Tasha heard a female voice say as she got of Jackson's car to go inside.

"You know what, Shantae?" I'm about sick and tired of you!" Tianna barked.

When Tianna was about to go upside Shantae's weaved head, Jackson jumped out of the car and grabbed Tianna to take her inside the house.

"That's right, you better take Blackie inside that house before I beat her black ass."

Shantae laughed along with her posse, Amber and Renee.

Neither Tianna nor Jackson said anything and continued walking. Jackson held onto and protected Tianna. But Shantae kept talking.

"You know what, Shantae? You ain't even worth it. You're not worth my time or energy!" Tianna said.

"That's right. You better take her inside, Jackson."

"Shantae, shut up and take your trifling ass somewhere else," Jackson said.

"Forget you, Jackson. You know you still want me."

"In your dreams." Jackson took his hand and shooed her away like she was a pesky gnat, and walked inside the house with Tianna.

Debby heard all the commotion in the front yard and walked downstairs to see what was going on. She met Jamal walking out of Tianna's room because he saw from the window that Shantae was out front causing trouble. He wanted to protect Tianna. Most importantly, he was going to get Tianna away from Jackson.

Jackson closed the front door and left Shantae talking to herself.

He asked Tianna if she was okay and told her to ignore Shantae because she was seeking attention and wouldn't be getting it from him.

He unexpectedly took Tianna in his arms and gave her a soft, sincere, and gentle hug to let her know that he would never let anyone harm her. He lifted her face to his with his fore and middle finger and placed a gentle kiss on top of her forehead, and then her cheek, followed by her nose, and lastly upon her lips.

"What in the hell is going on here?" Debby asked when she saw Jackson kiss Tianna.

"Yeah, I would like to know the same," Jamal said.

"Ummm, hi, Mrs. Thompson. I—I was making sure Tianna was all right." Jackson stuttered, moving away from Tianna.

"From my view, it looked like you were doing more than that! Tianna, what is going on with you and Jackson?"

"Nothing, Granny. Jackson brought me home," Tianna explained but her grandma cut her off, letting her know that she was there when she and Jamal first got home, and that she saw her leave with Jackson. She wanted to know what was going on between them and she wasn't taking "nothing" for an answer.

"Jackson, what the hell do you want with my granddaughter?"

"What is going on in here?" Bernadette walked into her home and saw and heard all the voices. Tianna was looking like a hot mess, like a volcano just hit her. Jamal and Jackson looked like they were in the boxing ring with Floyd Mayweather, but got their asses kicked.

"Mrs. Thompson, I'm going to be honest with you all. This may come as a shock, but I'm in *love* with your daughter." Jackson said.

"What?! The hell you ain't! Boy, if you don't get up out of here talking that nonsense. Tianna is going to finish her education. She ain't got time for no damn boys."

Jamal stood there in shock, wanting to beat Jackson's ass. How was he in love with his future wife? Jamal cleared his throat and looked directly into Tianna's eyes. He was searching for any signs of his feelings being reciprocated. She looked away from Jamal, unable to believe that Jackson stood there in front of him and her family expressing his feelings. She looked at Jackson with admiration and wanted to jump into his arms, but instead, she stayed reserved. She didn't want to hurt anyone, especially not Jamal or Tasha. Tianna had a ghostly look on her face as she turned to the doorway and saw Tasha standing there, witnessing as her brother expressed his true feelings for her best friend.

When Tasha saw the look on Tianna's face, she knew her feelings for Jackson were mutual. Tianna loved Jackson. She couldn't bear losing her friend and brother, so Tasha blasted back out the front door.

Tianna took off after her and so did Jackson.

"Tasha, wait. I can explain."

Tasha didn't stop. She sped up as the rain continued to pour down in buckets.

"Tashhhhhaaa!" Jackson called out to his sister, to no avail. She kept running.

Tasha turned on the street to her home, and that's when the sounds of squealing tires and a car horn were heard.

Errrrrr and Crasssssshhhhhhhhhh!!!!

"Tashhhhhha!" Tianna cried out.

"Tash!" Jackson cried

"Tashhhhhaaaaaa! Oh My God!"

"Somebody call an ambulance and quick!"

The tight-knit community all came outside to see a school bus and Coach Wilson's Ford Bronco collide, but Tasha could not be seen.

"Somebody help! *Please*!" A cry could be heard.

The sirens of the Emergency Medical System rang from a distance as the rain and lightning grew stronger.

Booommmm! The lightning struck and all the power in the entire community went dark. The only thing you could hear where mumbles and the sirens of the ambulance drawing close.

Chapter Nine

Oh my God! Where am I? Where are my mom and dad? All I remember is hearing Tianna and Jackson calling me. The lightning and rain distorting my vision along with my tears after seeing my best friend and my brother's intimate kiss. Where are they? My head hurts and I can't move. I see a bright flashing light, trees, and a forest with beautiful butterflies. That's a glorious rainbow. I can touch it. The smell of fresh pine trees and autumn invades my nostrils. I'm beginning to hear voices and beeping noises, but I can't understand what they are saying. Speak louder, I can't hear you. Where and who are you people? Please cut off that machine that keeps beeping. It sounds like an alarm. Am I late for school? If so, why hasn't Jackson come in to wake me? Where is he?

Jackson!

Mama!

Dad!

Where are you all?

Mr. and Mrs. Norwood, Jackson, Tianna, and Jamal crowded the room at University Hospital. Mrs. Norwood sat on the left side of Tasha's bed while her husband held onto his wife's hand, comforting her as she cried and prayed for her daughter lying in the trauma unit. Tasha was airlifted and flown immediately to the emergency room in critical condition. She had been struck by the school bus and Coach Wilson's SUV, flew up in the air, and landed on her backside. She suffered a broken collarbone, a broken leg, and a fractured skull with internal bleeding.

Dr. Anderson said that she was lucky to be alive.

Tasha was alive, but she was in a coma. It had been two years and she hadn't woken up.

She missed her senior year of high school and her first year of college.

Tianna was enrolled at Harvard University. Jackson accepted a scholarship to North Carolina University, and Jamal attended Duke University.

It was the holiday season and Tianna, Jackson, and Jamal were home on vacation. They always met at the hospital this time of year, ever since the accident, hoping and praying for Tasha to return. But each year, they left disappointed and sad that she still hadn't woken up.

Jackson longed for the day he and his sister would get on each other's nerves. He loved his sister and would do anything to be able to tease her again. But after he picked her up and gave her a thousand kisses, he would never let her go.

Tianna was currently enrolled in therapy to cope with the guilt after her best friend's accident. She blamed herself for what happened to Tasha. If she had stayed away from Jackson and not let her feelings for him come between them, Tasha would be here with her, not lying comatose in a hospital bed.

Tianna told Jackson that she couldn't be with him, even though she loved him. It would be heartless and scandalous if they were in a relationship. He was broken up about Tianna refusing to be with him, and accepted the scholarship to North Carolina to get far away from her and move on. But the distance only made him miss her more. He still loved Tianna and nothing or no one was going to change his heart.

Jamal would enter the NBA draft next season as the number one draft prospect. He had been secretly waiting for the day that Tasha returned from her coma so that he could propose marriage to Tianna. His heart hurt seeing Tianna devastated by the accident. She lost so much weight, became very depressed, and had to enter into the best therapy program that money could buy. She had come a long way to get back to normal. Soon after Tasha's accident, Tianna had to be talked off the ledge of a department store building. She wanted to end her life. She couldn't bear her life without her friend. They had known each other since they were five years old. Tasha was a yin to her yang. She was pepper to her pepper, since they both were copper colored. She loved her more than her life. She was her true sister since Tianna was an only child.

The Norwoods embraced Tianna and didn't blame her or Jackson for what happened to their only daughter. They knew that Tianna would never do anything to hurt Tasha and that it was an unfortunate accident.

Tianna often visited the Norwoods for small talk, but the home was not the same without Tasha's sassy and bubbly personality. Jackson was away at college, and she was happy that she didn't have to see him. They saw each other each year at the hospital at Tasha's bedside.

Each year Jackson saw Tianna, he reminisced about having her in his arms. He hadn't been with any other girl since Tasha's accident. He waited for Tianna.

He looked at her from across the hospital room and noticed that she had gained her weight back and decided to grow dreadlocks. She was so beautiful with a brown knitted hat that sat on top of her locs. She wore big hoop earrings that accented her attire. She wore brown three-inch Gucci boots that made her five feet nine inches, instead of five feet six inches tall. She rocked natural well.

Tianna caught Jackson staring at her and quickly sipped her hot chocolate. It was a cold winter in Texas and it had been snowing for a few days. This was unusual for San Antonio, Texas because it hadn't snowed since 2001.

Jamal walked to Tianna and asked if she needed him to go get her anything. Tianna declined and said that she was fine. He went around the room asking if anyone needed anything because he was headed to the cafeteria to grab a bite to eat.

The Norwoods and Jackson didn't need anything.

Jackson wondered why Jamal was visiting, but didn't say anything. It was not the time to get into it with Jamal. His primary concern was his sister and he didn't want anything or anyone stopping her from waking up. He let Jamal slide for the time being, so he played his cordial role to perfection. He even shook Jamal's hand upon seeing him.

Tianna was happy to see Jackson and Jamal quash their high school beef. They were young *adults* in college and shouldn't continue their childish antics. They were both expected to be in the NBA next season. Jamal was a sure bet, but Jackson was not. Jackson was going to school to become a pharmacist in case his professional basketball career failed. He had a back-up plan for Tianna and him. The only problem was, Jamal planned for him and Tianna too. Tianna on the other hand, wasn't planning for either of them.

Tianna met a guy in one of her law classes and was dating him. No one knew of Tianna's significant other and she kept it that way. When her mother and grandmother came to visit, she made sure that her male companion was not around until they left.

Tianna had been dating Mark for about six months and their relationship was exclusive and serious. She met his parents, Mark White Sr. and Samantha White, and they absolutely loved her and offered her a full-time paid intern job at their law firm. She accepted and had been learning how to become a trial lawyer. Tianna hadn't decided yet if she wanted to be a prosecutor or defender, but her long-term goal was to become a judge.

Mark was a twin to his sister, Markette and they were both in a position to take over their parents' law firm once they retired.

Markette was a spoiled brat, according to Mark. She had always been a daddy's girl. Mark and his father, Mark Sr. never really had a cohesive father and son relationship. He often wondered why his mother named him after his father because he was *nothing* like him. His father was an arrogant asshole who treated people like crap. He was one of the best attorneys in Boston, Massachusetts because he was ruthless. Many people referred to him as a brother from another mother of Johnny Cochran when it came to trying cases and winning. He won them all. Guilty or not was not his concern, winning was the name of *his* game. He was also a habitual gambler.

Mrs. White kept a separate financial account from her husband because of his excessive gambling. They had been married for twenty-five years, but only five years of the marriage was happy. After the children, her husband changed. The outside world didn't know what was going on inside the White's household and the family kept it *their* secret. To the outside world looking in, they looked like the perfect, successful, and happy upscale family. They fooled everyone, including Tianna. She had no idea who she was working for or was involved with romantically.

Tianna's phone rang and she answered and told Mark to hold on. She stepped outside Tasha's room to acquire some privacy to talk to her *Boo*. Mark talked about missing her and how he couldn't wait for her to return. He went by her apartment to feed her parrot Pauline, who was very talkative. The parrot was a delight to be around, but she was a loud mouth. She told all Tianna's business to Mark. He didn't even have to ask. The minute he walked into Tianna's two-bedroom, comfy, huge apartment located in Boston, near the downtown area, Pauline said, "She was crying about Tasha, *again*."

Mark let Pauline know that Tianna was gone to visit Tasha and that she would be gone for another week.

Pauline repeated,

"She was crying about Tasha, again."

Mark sighed and continued to feed Pauline. He adored Pauline and he and Tianna would hold a full conversation with her as if she was a human being.

One day, Mark came over to visit Tianna, and Pauline blurted out, "Tianna *loves* Jackson."

Mark and Tianna had just begun dating when Pauline made Mark aware of Jackson.

Pauline telling Tianna's business was so bad that Tianna threatened to put a muzzle on her mouth if she didn't keep quiet. Pauline promised to keep her mouth shut, but it didn't last for long periods of time.

The first three months of Mark and Tianna's relationship, Mark continued to hear Pauline say, "Tianna *loves* Jackson."

Once Pauline got to know Mark, she never said it again. But Mark didn't know if it was because of Tianna's threat or if Pauline was finally embracing him. He wished it was the latter and not the former, but he had a feeling it was Tianna's threat.

Mark stayed with Pauline for a few minutes and then he left. He felt bad leaving Pauline alone, but if he took her from Tianna's apartment she would talk non-stop, causing many sleepless nights for him. Mark had tried to keep Pauline before while Tianna was away, and had to bring her back home to her cage. He *never* volunteered to take Pauline home again.

Mark assured Tianna that Pauline was fine and that she told him that she was crying about Tasha. Tianna sighed and didn't want to threaten Pauline with the muzzle over the phone. She missed her and couldn't wait to get back home to Pauline and her Boo, but she needed to spend time with her best friend, mother, and grandmother. She hadn't seen them since their last visit to Boston.

Tianna's father was more involved in his daughter's life than before. He often sent her money for groceries. He visited once when she first moved to Cambridge to attend Harvard and often bragged about her. He recently had another child by a woman who he was engaged to. Tianna's little brother was named Tyrell Malik Jones, but T.J is what everyone called him. Tianna loved her baby brother, who was learning to walk when she last saw him. His skin complexion was the same as Tianna's, a smooth and silky chocolate.

Jamal walked back to Tasha's room after being gone for over thirty minutes at the hospital's cafeteria. He saw Tianna talking on the phone. He overheard her say, "I miss you too, baby."

Jamal scowled and mimicked, "baby." He thought to himself, *Who the hell is she talking to?*

Tianna gave kisses to Mark through the phone.

When she pressed end on her iPhone, she turned around and bumped into Jamal staring at her with a scowl on his face.

"Oh, hey, Jamal." She didn't know what to say, or if he'd overheard her conversation with Mark.

"Who were you talking to?" Jamal asked as if she was his wife and she needed to answer to him.

"I was talking to a friend."

"A friend with benefits?" Jamal questioned.

"Jamal, you are out of line and that's none of your business."

"Tianna, we will always have unfinished business between us, so technically, it is *my* business."

"Jamal, please, let's not do this here."

"Do what here?" Jackson asked as he walked outside Tasha's room to check on Tianna.

Tianna and Jamal looked at Jackson and then at each other. They didn't say anything because no one knew about their *one-time* kiss. Well, they thought no one knew, but Jackson knew. He knew about them locking lips in her room back in high school. In fact, he never got over the visual. Each time he saw Jamal, it took all his restraint not to put him in the hospital. He didn't want to kill him, but he wanted to hurt him *real* bad.

"Dr. Anderson! Can someone please page Dr. Anderson! My daughter squeezed my finger! My daughter squeezed my finger! Oh my God! Tasha squeezed my finger, Jackson. She can hear me," Mrs. Norwood cried in Jackson's arms.

They all walked back into Tasha's room.

Tasha began to blink her eyes and clear her throat. Dr. Anderson smiled and examined her. He called for the nurse to get Tasha some water and instructed her to sit Tasha upright and take her vitals.

"Tasha, can you hear me? If you can hear me, I want you to nod your head."

Tasha began to nod her head.

Tianna screamed, "Tasha, I love you! Come back to me!"

Tasha opened her eyes to see her friend and she began to speak. "Girllll, what the heck did you do to your hair?"

Everyone busted out laughing because Tasha Norwood was back! Tianna had a natural thick Afro before the accident, but now she had dreadlocks. Tasha was never a fan of dreadlocks, but she loved the way they looked on her best friend.

"I need some water. I'm thirsty and it seems like I haven't had a drink in years."

Tasha continued to clear her throat.

"That's because you haven't had any water in years, Big Head." Jackson said as he came up and gave Tasha a grandiose genuine hug. He held her tight and didn't let go.

"What's the matter with you? You miss me or something? Why you hugging all over me?"

Tasha had so many questions and jokes that made Christmas Eve a day to remember.

This was the best blessing and gift anyone could ask for.

The Norwoods got their daughter back.
Tianna got her best friend back.
Jackson and Jamal vowed to get Tianna back.

Chapter Ten

Please Come Home for Christmas, played in the background.

The smell of pumpkin spice enveloped the entire Norwood home. The pinewood Christmas tree that sat in the front window stood eleven feet tall. Neighbors had stalked the tree ever since Mr. Norwood put it up three weeks ago.

Gifts galore sat underneath the tree and on top of the hardwood floors.

Tasha sat in a wheelchair next to the tree looking out the window. Her mother watched her from the kitchen while she prepared Christmas dinner. She couldn't believe her daughter was *finally* home.

Tasha made a miraculous recovery and was set to be back on her feet within two weeks. Tasha wanted to enroll in a program to get her GED and then enroll at Texas A&M University to become a child psychologist. Prior to her accident, she wanted to be a make-up artist, but her near-death experience had given her a change of heart.

Jackson came down the stairway and saw his sister sitting by the window. He came up from behind her and hugged and kissed her on the top of the forehead.

"You know I love you, right?" he said as he smiled and looked into her dark brown eyes.

"Ewwwwww, boy quit. I don't want you kissing all over me." She laughed and pushed him away.

"Awwww, Big Head. I'm glad you are home. I missed you," he said as he continued to kiss all over her.

"Stopppp, Jackson."

She said "stop," meaning, don't stop, but Tasha didn't want her brother to know how much she loved him. She called out to her mother to come get him.

"Jackson, leave your sister alone."

"Nope, she's my gift from God and I'm never going to leave her again," he said as he gave her head a slight push.

"Merry Christmas, Tasha."

"Merry Christmas," she responded.

"Are you picking up Tianna and bringing her here?" Tasha inquired.

"Yeah, what time?"

"She said at around twelve noon, but I will call her to make sure."

"Bet. I'm going to run an errand and then I'll pick her up."

"Jackson, I want you to behave yourself in front of the guests."

"Mama, I ain't a teenager anymore. I'm a *grown* man." He gave his mother a kiss as he grabbed an apple from the fruit basket that sat on the table.

"All right, *grown man*, you better be on your best grown man behavior and not embarrass your dad or me."

"Bye, Mama."

"Be careful, and dinner starts at one p.m."

Jackson slammed the door like he always did, as if he didn't have ears to hear how hard he slammed it.

Tasha sat and looked outside at a semi-winter Christmas. It was thirty-seven degrees and a cold front was due in the area at around three p.m. Temperatures were expected to drop below freezing.

The local weather services gave warnings to bring pets and plants inside, and limit the roadways because there could be ice flurries.

The warning to cover all water pipes in the house or let the water drip to keep them from freezing scrolled at the bottom of the television screen.

"Mama, you need any help? I know I'm in this wheelchair, but there's nothing wrong with my hands."

"You can come and peel these potatoes."

Tasha was delighted that her mother let her wheel herself into the kitchen to make herself handy. Her mother usually didn't allow anyone in the kitchen during Christmas or Thanksgiving. She didn't want people messing up her recipes, so she did it all.

Well, almost all. Jackson and Tasha had always shared kitchen duties once the guests left.

The doorbell rang and Mr. Norwood answered and let a few members from the church inside. Sharon's brother and sister, along with their kids came shortly after. Sharon had lost her mother to breast cancer six years ago.

Mr. Norwood's family arrived and began their holiday ritual, watching sports and gambling on the games.

"Merry Christmas!" Adonis's mother, Anita sang. In fact, she was happy her name was Anita because she sang so much that people called her Anita Baker.

"Merry Christmas, Mama," Adonis said as he kissed his mother's left cheek.

"You gaining a little weight, ain't cha, son? It's that good cooking from Sharon, huh?" she teased as she patted Adonis's belly.

"Merry Christmas, Sharon. I see you're taking real good care of my son."

Sharon smiled as she hugged her mother-in-law.

Adonis's mother was very protective of her son and when he planned to marry Sharon, she thought that they were rushing and too young. She loved Sharon and her family, but Adonis and Sharon had just graduated high school when he proposed to her and she accepted. Adonis was going into the military, and before he left he wanted to make sure that Sharon would always be his girl, so he married her. They had been married for twenty-two years, and had the perfect marriage and family. Adonis was a good faithful man that loved his wife, and the feelings were reciprocated. They both came from two-parent households and knew what it took to raise wholesome kids. Jackson and Tasha were both ideal children. Jackson was in college, and Tasha would have been in college too if it wasn't for her accident.

"Merry Christmas, Tasha. How are you sweetie?"

"Grandma, I'm fine. I'm thankful and fortunate to be here. Although, I don't remember much of anything that happened before the accident or why I was running. My memory comes and goes," Tasha explained.

No one mentioned why Tasha was running away that day or what she saw that caused her to run into the street and get struck by the school bus and Mr. Wilson's SUV. The Norwoods were not aware of the reasons Tasha was running away, but Jackson, Tianna, and Jamal knew why. They didn't want to say because it happened over two years ago, and they were all happy to have Tasha return to them.

Tasha would give anything to have her memory back, but she had no recollection of Jackson and Tianna's affair and they wanted to leave it that way. Tianna knew that Tasha would never accept her as anything but her best friend, never a sister-in-law.

Tianna wanted to be in Jackson's arms, his lips kissing her, but her friendship was more important and she wanted to keep it that way for the meantime.

Oh shoot, it's almost time for Jackson to come. I must hurry because I know that he will be on that horn like a crazy man and if Mama was home, she would come outside and curse him out. She doesn't care if it's Christmas Day or not. Thankfully, Mama is at work. She doesn't particularly care for Jackson, but she doesn't hate him either, she just preferred Jamal. She thinks of Jackson as a playa, and out to get her daughter pregnant and then leave for the NBA. Mama has always admired Jamal's mannerism, his clean cut and sparkling personality. She knew Jamal was a shoo-in to the NBA too and could take care of me. Mama must stop treating me like a little girl. I'm a grown woman now, I'm in college, and falling in love with Mark.

Tianna tried to reason with her feelings by telling herself that she was in love with Mark. In reality, she had deep feelings for him, but it was nowhere on the level of her feelings for Jackson. Mark was like Sweet'N Low, and Jackson was the real thing, sugar. Pure cane *brown* sugar. It had been over two years since her *brief* love affair with Jackson, but she was not over him. She thought about him every day. When she hugged Mark, she thought about Jackson. When she kissed Mark, she envisioned kissing Jackson. Everything intimate she did with Mark, it was Jackson in her mind.

Tianna heard a horn blow, not once, but twice. She looked out her bedroom window and saw Jackson. She smiled like it was picture day at school. She grabbed her Gucci Bloom perfume and sprayed it all over her and put on her coat. She had given her grandmother and mother their Christmas gifts earlier. Her mother had to work on Christmas, so there was no Christmas dinner at the Thompson household. Tianna wanted to surprise her mother at work by bringing her some of Sharon's homemade cooking.

Tianna rushed downstairs and found her grandmother in the kitchen making some lunch. She wished her a Merry Christmas and kissed her goodbye. Grandma Debby looked forward to spending time with Tianna since she was only home for two weeks before she returned to school. She couldn't believe how Tianna had changed since she left home. Her grandbaby had grown up so beautifully, inside and out. She knew that Tianna loved Jackson and he loved her. Grandma Debby would never stand in the way of her granddaughter's happiness.

Jackson saw Tianna come outside and lock the front door. He hopped out of the car to open her door. He couldn't believe they were together again. He wanted to swoop her up and kiss her and take her to his bedroom. He refrained because he was waiting for her.

"Merry Christmas, Jackson."

"Merry Christmas," Jackson said as he pulled out a sprig of mistletoe from his coat and held it over Tianna's head.

"Oh noooo, you didn't," she said and smiled.

She heard and felt her phone ring, looked at the screen, and saw that it was Mark. She answered after the third ring.

"Hey, babe. How are you?" Tianna asked enthusiastically.

"I'm missing you. I wish you weren't away."

"I know, but once I return, you will have me all to yourself."

Jackson closed Tianna's car door as she got in the car talking to her *Boo.* Jackson was not only jealous, he felt violated. He was trying to win Tianna back, but she was on the phone calling another man *"babe."* He turned up his nose and wanted to take her phone and hang it up. Instead, he started the car and turned on *her* song.

"Let me know."

Tianna looked into Jackson's eyes and she quickly turned away. She wished Mark a Merry Christmas and told him that she would call him later.

Mark asked what the noise in the background was, and who was playing *her* song? Tianna said nothing; she was too busy thinking of her and Jackson kissing.

"I'll call you later," she insisted and pushed the end button on her iPhone.

"That's right. Tell that fool, bye!"

"Did you play that song on purpose, Jackson?"

"Yes, I did, because this is *our* song. Now, where were we before we were rudely interrupted?" Jackson held the mistletoe over Tianna's head and reached over to kiss her lips. She didn't resist or object. Instead, she met him halfway and their lips did their familiar dance. Jackson leaned in even more to devour her tongue and he couldn't resist cupping her breast with one hand as Tianna's hat hit the car floor. He couldn't get enough of her and she couldn't get enough of him.

"Jackson, please." Tianna tried to gasp for air, but he wouldn't' let her. He'd waited two years for this moment and he wasn't going to waste a minute of it. He had to let her know how much he loved and missed her.

"Tianna, I love you," he continuously said as he kissed her. Say you love me, too. *Please*."

"Jackson, I love you too, but I can't," she said with tears in her eyes.

He saw her tears and asked "why?" He would never stop loving her. He had tried, but it hadn't helped because she was all that he thought about for years.

She felt the same way, but it could never be, and the reason was Tasha. She had just been released from the hospital and there was no need to hamper her recovery. They had their entire lives, and the number one priority was keeping their love for one another a secret. She would never do anything to hurt her best friend.

"Tianna, are you going to live your life for you or for others?" Jackson asked.

"Jackson, this isn't about me. This is bigger than us."

"Oh, really? I get it, you want to be with your *Boo*. I get it. I won't sweat you no more. If that's who you want to be with."

"No, it's not like that."

"Then what the hell is it, Tianna? Do you know how long I've waited to have you in my arms again? Huh?"

"Jackson, it's complicated. You don't understand. What about everybody we will hurt?"

"We ain't hurtin' nobody but ourselves. I ain't living for other people. I'm living my life and want to live it with you. Goddammit! What's so wrong about that?"

Tianna didn't say anything. She couldn't. Jackson took his thumb and wiped her tears and then kissed them and looked into her eyes,

"I'm never going to give you up!" he said as he started the car and headed to his parent's house for Christmas dinner.

Chapter Eleven

Tianna and Jackson arrived at his home, and as they walked inside, there was Christmas music playing, and the television was on the NBA basketball game. The children were playing, and pots and pans could be heard in the kitchen. The men sat inside the man cave to watch the Los Angeles Lakers play the San Antonio Spurs. It was Kobe Bryant against Tim Duncan. Tianna glanced at the television. The Spurs were leading the Lakers by four points and it was still only the first half.

"Tiannnnnaa!" Tasha squealed as she saw her best friend enter the living room. She couldn't get over to her fast enough, so Tianna met her in the middle of the kitchen and they hugged for what seemed like hours. They didn't want to let each other go. Tasha was the first to break the embrace.

"You look and smell good, girl! I hope Jackson wasn't giving you any trouble. You know how my brother can be."

"No, he was a gentleman and on his best behavior," Tianna confessed.

"Tasha, I'm always a gentleman and on my best behavior. Ain't that right, Mama?" Jackson wanted his mother to chime in, but she didn't pay him any mind. She was too busy greeting Tianna and wishing her a Merry Christmas. She took Tianna's coat to hang it on the coat rack. She asked Tianna about her fragrance and how it smelled so good. Tianna gave her the name, cost, and where she purchased her Gucci Bloom perfume.

"Hi, darling," Anita sang as she hugged and kissed Tianna.

"Grandma, this is Tianna. You remember her? It's been a while since you have seen her because she's at Harvard University."

"Yes, I know Tianna. She hasn't changed much, only her hair has these worms in them," she said as she fiddled with one of Tianna's locs.

"Grandma, they are dreadlocks," Tasha explained but Anita turned up her nose with a sigh.

"I don't know why people want to let their hair knot up like that," Anita said.

The doorbell rang as soon as Anita was about to start preaching about dreadlocks. Tianna was saved by the bell.

Mr. Norwood opened the door and in walked Darren and Jamal. Tianna thought to herself, *what is Jamal doing here?* She didn't know he was invited to Christmas dinner. She gave her hair a one-finger fix and cleared her throat.

When Jackson saw Jamal he couldn't believe he was here at his house for Christmas and wondered who invited him. The look on his face said everything about how he felt, but again, he didn't want to show his ass on Christmas day and he'd already been warned several times about being on his *best* behavior.

Darren walked over to Tasha to give her a long hug and a kiss. He was a good guy and stayed by Tasha's side throughout her accident and recovery. He would read literature and pray for her each day. Although he wasn't at the hospital the day Tasha woke up from her coma. He never forgave himself for not being there at that moment.

He worked with his father, who owned his own software company, so he could come and go as he pleased. He brought fresh flowers and teddy bears weekly for two years. Tasha had donated her stuffed animals to the children's hospital.

Jamal wished Tianna a Merry Christmas and unexpectedly kissed her smack on her lips. Tianna was shocked and it caught her off guard. Once he was done kissing Tianna, he looks directly into her eyes and licked his sexy lips.

Jamal didn't look the same as he had in high school, he was sexier. His hair had waves deeper than the Atlantic Ocean. His arms were masculine and muscular. Solid, but not too bulky. His butt cheeks were perky like cantaloupes.

"Merry Christmas, Jamal," Tianna whispered after she caught her breath.

"Merry Christmas, beautiful."

Jamal still called Tianna "beautiful" after all these years. She blushed inside and out. Who said that dark-skinned people can't blush? Tianna clearly turned a reddish hue.

"Hey, Jamal. Thank you for coming and Merry Christmas," Tasha said as she embraced him with a warm holiday hug.

"I'm so glad to see you. I could pick you up and kiss you," Jamal said.

Throughout the last two years when Jamal was home on vacation, he often visited Tasha in the hospital. He would keep Darren company, and they often sat in the room to talk about sports. They would play NBA 2k12. Jamal was fortunate enough to be at the hospital when Tasha came out of her coma. Tasha could remember all her friends and family, but she could not remember how or why she'd been in an accident. She had no recollection of her brother and best friend's romantic involvement, nor did she know anything about the kiss that Jamal and Tianna shared. Or the reason Jackson and Jamal had a fight.

Jackson gave Darren a friendly handshake and reluctantly did the same with Jamal. He invited them into the man cave to watch the NBA game. He also wanted to get Jamal away from Tianna and keep an eye on him. You know what they say, "Keep your friends close and your enemies closer."

Jamal wasn't Jackson's enemy, but they were not friends. They were associates.

Associates in love with the same woman.

"Man, Kobe is such a ball hog!" Jamal shouted after Kobe passed up a wide-open Pau Gasol.

"He's the GOAT, though," Darren said.

"Yeah, I see you taking up for your man crush," Jackson laughed.

"Jealous, fellas," Darren teased.

"Look at him. He had Jordan Clarkson open and still shot an off balance three pointer. Now, they are down by ten points because of that ball hog," Jamal said, continuing his attack on Kobe. Besides, Jamal was a Spurs fan and hoped to be drafted by Greg Popovich. Tony Parker would be retired in a few years and Jamal could take his place in his dream, as well as his reality. He truly believed that he had a chance to be a part of the best organization in basketball.

The sports talk between the fellas became heated, but the smell of Mrs. Sharon's cooking and the sound of her voice telling everyone the food was ready cooled them off and caused a different type of uproar. One that caused them to make a beeline to the main dining room.

Tianna helped Tasha get situated at the table and she sat to the right side of her. Darren sat on Tasha's left side.

Jackson sat directly in front of Tianna while Jamal sat on the right side of Tianna. There was a lot of small talk on how good the food was and chatter about Tasha's miraculous recovery but everyone wanted to get back to the game and others had family to visit.

The holiday meal ended and some of the guests began to go back to the man cave, while others were leaving to visit other family members.

Mrs. Norwood walked her church member guests to the door to bid them farewell.

Tasha, Tianna, and Jackson remained in the kitchen to make leftover plates and to clean up.

Tianna asked Jackson if he could take her to give her mom a plate. Jamal overheard Tianna and offered to take her, but Jackson quickly disapproved and told him he "got it." Jamal insisted, and said that he was on his way out and wouldn't mind giving Tianna a ride to wherever she needed to go.

Tasha put her two cents in and advocated for Jamal to take Tianna wherever she needed. She wanted to spend time with her brother, but didn't know how to tell him.

Jackson wasn't backing down. He went to the coat rack to acquire Tianna's coat. He helped her put it on, took her hand, and told everyone that he would see them later.

Tasha was shocked and wanted to know what was going on between her brother and best friend. Tianna said nothing because deep down inside she wanted Jackson to take her.

Jamal tried to intervene, but to no avail. Jackson and Tianna bid everyone farewell and were out the door before he could protest further.

"Damn, Jamal doesn't take no for an answer," Jackson hissed as he opened the car door for Tianna.

"It wasn't that serious, Jackson."

"I know it isn't to him, but it is for me."

"Why is that?"

"I think we both know why. I want you and I don't care about your little boyfriend or Jamal. I've lost you before and I won't let it happen again."

"Jackson, stop. Don't do this."

"Do what, Tianna? Huh? You want me to go away?"

"No, that's not what I'm saying."

"I know you're not, because I know you want me as much as I want you. I got a gift for you, too, but I didn't want to give it to you in front of everyone."

Jackson pulled out a small gift box wrapped in gold wrapping paper with a green bow.

He handed it to Tianna. She looked down at how beautifully wrapped it was and asked what it was. He told her that he wasn't telling and to open it. She opened it carefully. Tianna couldn't believe her eyes. Her hands were shaking as she looked down and saw a beautiful heart necklace with the initials JN & TT engraved on the back. The initials stood for Jackson Norwood and Tianna Thompson.

Jackson put the necklace around her neck. After he was done fastening the clasp, Tianna leaned in to give Jackson a kiss and mouthed, "Thank you." She flipped down the sun visor to look in the mirror and see how it looked on her. It was perfect because it was from *Jackson*.

Jackson started the car and they drove to Tianna's mother's job at the hospital where she worked as a Licensed Vocational Nurse. She gave her mother her plate and wished her a Merry Christmas. She and Jackson stopped in town to listen to the Christmas carolers, and watch the Christmas lights.

They talked about their aspirations and her living in Boston.

Jackson knew that he couldn't ask her to move back to Texas, but made plans to come and visit her once basketball season ended.

"What about Mark?" She asked.

"What about him?"

"Jackson, I can't leave him."

"Why not? You don't love him."

"It's complicated and you wouldn't understand."

Tianna was right. Jackson didn't know how much Mark and his family had done for her and her career. There's a lot that Jackson didn't know about Mark that Tianna didn't want to discuss. The fact that her family hadn't met Mark, and the reason why Tianna had never introduced Mark to her family.

Tianna's phone rang and it was Mark. She answered.

"Hey, you."

Jackson hissed and motioned for Tianna to hang up the phone. Tianna ignored him and continued talking to her Boo.

"I miss you, too," Tianna said and sent smooches through her phone as she ended the call.

"*I miss you, too.*" Jackson said, mimicking her voice. He reeked of jealousy and sarcasm.

Tianna couldn't help but laugh. She gave Jackson a kiss and asked if he was jealous. He asked what she thought, and she continued to laugh because she thought it was cute.

"Oh, you think it's funny?" he said as he grabbed her and started tickling her. "I'm going to give you something to laugh about."

"Stop, Jackson."

"Nawww, you think me being jealous is funny," he said as he continued tickling her. She opened the car door to escape from him. She stood outside the car to catch her breath.

Jackson walked around to Tianna's side of the car. He leaned against her, cupped her face with both hands, and kissed her passionately. He whispered into her mouth, "I love you," over and over. Their bodies began to crave each other, but Tianna had a boyfriend. How could she cheat on him? She cared for Mark, though she didn't love him the way she loved Jackson.

Jackson picked her up and spun her around until she was dizzy. They were like high school kids. He hugged her from the back, leaned against his car, and whispered in her ear.

"I want you to be mine," he said as he nibbled on her ear.

Tianna was in awe. She couldn't believe the man that she'd wanted since high school was holding her in his arms and asking her to be his woman.

She didn't answer. Instead, she closed her eyes and envisioned a life with him. He continued holding her tight and not letting go. They watched the lights for another hour and then headed to Tianna's house.

"I'm going to walk you inside to make sure you're safe."

Tianna nodded okay without saying a word. He walked around to open her door and picked her up in his arms. Her hat fell to the ground, but neither she nor he cared. He was too busy embracing her with his unspoken words.

She opened her pocket purse to retrieve the key to unlock the door. Jackson entered the house and carried her up the stairs and into her room.

It was dark, but Tianna guided him with her iPhone light. Her hands wrapped around his neck and her head lay on his right shoulder. She opened the door to her bedroom and he gently laid her down on her bed.

He took her coat off and removed her boots. He began to rub her feet as she relaxed in a euphoric trance. He lay softly on top of her and searched her dark brown beaded eyes. He looks directly into them, searching for a reaction for what was about to happen.

He looked for signs of resistance, but there were none.

He kissed her lips and removed her blouse until she was only wearing her bra. He continued to read her signals and nothing but a green light was registering. He unzipped her miniskirt and placed it on the floor. He removed her bra, and finally, her strawberry-red colored thong.

Tianna's heart was running a marathon, but she wasn't out of breath, it was from excitement.

He continued to devour her lips and moved down to her neck, and then shoulder.

Tianna mumbled, "Ooooohhhh, Jackson," in a raspy, sultry monotone.

"You love me?" he asked as his lips kissed her perky breasts.

He didn't get an answer, so he moved to her left breast and asked again.

"Do you love me?"

Tianna arched her back and whispered,

"Yes, Jackson, I do *love* you."

Chapter Twelve

I knew my memory wasn't playing tricks on me. Tasha thought as she watched her brother and best friend outside her home as they sat in the car.

Tasha saw Jackson give Tianna the necklace and put it around her neck. She saw the kiss afterwards before they drove off.

She had been having short-term flashbacks of what happened to her before the accident. But the scenes were coming in short bursts. She remembered Jackson and Tianna kissing at school at her locker, Jackson telling her that he loved Tianna, and the pouring rain. She remembered running in the rain, but didn't remember what she was running from or to. She didn't know whether to confront Tianna or let her friend be happy with her brother.

I mean, she loves him and he clearly loves her, but would I lose my best friend and brother at the same time if they were to hook-up? Or should I approve of their relationship because it seems as if they have already hooked-up? I love them and I want the best for both, but I don't want to lose them, Tasha thought, fearing the loss and emptiness.

There was a knock on Tasha's bedroom door and it was her father. He asked if she needed anything before turning in for the night. She wished him a good night with a kiss and he closed the door behind him.

Tasha declined her father's generosity because she wanted to practice getting her strength back. Each night, she transferred herself in and out of the wheelchair, and would place the wheelchair to the side of her bed and try to walk. She worked hard to get her strength back. She could walk twelve steps, but no more than twelve, and would get tired and have to sit down. No one knew that she could walk because she wanted to surprise them at dinner, so she kept it a secret.

One night when Tasha was taking steps, she heard a knock on her door and it was her mother. Sharon almost caught her in the act, but Tasha sat down just in time. Tasha was strong willed, hard headed, and resilient. There was no way it would take her two weeks to get back to normal. All she needed was two days, and she worked hard daily. She planned to enroll in Texas A&M by the fall. Tasha specifically wanted to pursue the field of child psychology. She didn't quite give up the hair stylist dream, but she felt that children needed her assistance more.

Tasha's iPhone beeped. It was a missed call from Darren.

She wondered why her phone didn't ring, so she looked on the side of her phone and saw that her ringer was off. She called him back and they talked for about ten minutes and made plans to go to lunch tomorrow.

"You know I love you," Darren crooned into the phone.

"I know, and you better because I love you, too."

This was the first time that she had ever told Darren her true feelings. She would always show him love, but would only say, "me too" when he told her his sentiments of love.

"Are you getting soft on me?" Darren asked.

"Boy, please," Tasha said as she rolled her eyes until she almost fell asleep.

Darren laughed in his deep baritone voice. He wished her a goodnight and said he couldn't wait to see her tomorrow.

When Tasha hung up with Darren, she scrolled through her phone contacts and stopped at Tianna's name and phone number. She sat there looking at Tianna's profile picture, wondering if she should call and confront her about her brother. But was she ready to end her longtime friendship? Her brother was off-limits, even though she and Tianna never discussed Jackson. She didn't think Tianna would ever be attracted to her brother or vice versa. Tianna and Jackson had always cracked jokes on each other, and Tasha wouldn't have thought in a million years that they would become a couple.

Speaking of Tianna, an earlier text message from her vibrated through Tasha's iPhone that read:

Tianna: Hey, Tasha, if you are not busy tomorrow, I'd like to come by and go to the mall.

Tasha read the message.

She thought long and hard before she responded. It was time for Tianna to come clean about her brother or she was going to make her.

Tasha didn't know how to feel because it was none of her business what Jackson and Tianna did. But she still feared losing her friend and brother, so she didn't want them together. If that made any sense at all.

Tasha texted Tianna back and made plans to meet.

Chapter Thirteen

Jackson entered Jared's Jewelry Store. He walked to the area where the women's engagement rings were located. He saw a three-carat French-set diamond band with surprise diamonds. It featured a beautifully colorless diamond. The best money could buy. He didn't look at the price; he just wanted to know if they had a size six.

The jeweler assisted Jackson. He gave him the correct ring size and placed it in a ring box. Jackson paid cash for the ring because he had an inheritance from his late grandmother. He walked out of the store.

He got into his car and made a quick stop at a flower shop to purchase a dozen white roses. As Jackson walked out of the flower shop, he noticed through a glass window, Tianna and his sister sitting at the local café, eating and talking. He didn't go and speak to them because he didn't want Tianna to see the flowers that he planned to surprise her with that night.

While trying to duck and dodge Tianna and Tasha, Jackson ran right into Jamal. Jackson looked at Jamal between his tilted Gucci sunshades and let out a sigh. Jamal ignored his annoying sigh and apologized.

"So, who's the lucky lady?" Jamal asked.

"Someone you wouldn't know," Jackson responded.

"Bet?" Jamal shrugged.

"Bet?" Jackson said as he walked away from Jamal, trying to hide from Tianna.

Jamal wanted to continue to question Jackson, but he knew that he wasn't getting any answers, so he let it go. As he walked away he noticed Tianna and Tasha at the café.

He started calling Tianna's name from across the street.

Jackson couldn't believe it. He thought Jamal was about to blow his cover. He walked rapidly and discreetly until he reached his car. He used the flowers to hide his face.

*That damn Jamal with his big ass mouth almost got me caught. I got away just in time before Tianna saw me with **her** flowers. I plan to invite her to the house tonight for dinner and propose to her in front of my family. I hope she likes the ring and says YES!*

"Tianna!" Jamal continued to say and waved to catch her attention.

Tianna turned to see Jamal waving at her and calling her name. She waved back with an enormous smile.

"Oooh, who you cheesing at?" Tasha asked.

"Jamal, he's across the street by the flower shop."

Jamal crossed the street and walked to the café. He went to get an extra chair from another table and placed it next to Tianna and Tasha.

"How you doing, beautiful?" Jamal asked as he placed his lips on the left side of Tianna's check. "Hey Tasha, you're looking good. It's good to see you out."

"What are you doing down here? I thought you left town already?"

"Nah, I leave next week. When are you leaving?"

"I haven't quite decided yet. I keep changing my mind, *daily*. I know my parrot, Pauline, is missing me."

"What about your, Boo?" Tasha asked.

Tianna really didn't want to talk about Mark, especially in front of Jamal. She and Mark got into a little argument the other night because Tianna hadn't called him all day or night. Because she was with Jackson.

"He's a big boy. He can take care of himself until I return."

"Yeahh, right. You know these men act like kids and need their mamas," Tasha teased as she placed her left thumb in her mouth like a baby.

Jamal huffed, saying that he didn't need his mama, but that he was a mama's boy and proud of it. He let it be known to everyone how much he loved his mother and that he didn't have a problem being called a mama's boy. In fact, he was *proud* of it.

"Tianna, what are you doing later tonight? You want to get together and go bowling?" Jamal asked.

"Tasha, you want to go?"

Jamal didn't mind Tasha going, but he was asking Tianna out on a date on the cool and wanted some alone time with her before they both left town.

"Girl, naw, does it look like I can bowl?"

"They got five-pound bowling balls that you can bowl with," Tianna advised.

"No, and that's my final answer. Besides, you and Jamal can get caught up before you both return to school."

Tasha wasn't slick. She was trying to get Tianna and Jamal together so that her brother would be excluded as Tianna's love interest.

Jamal didn't object to Tasha turning down the invitation, and Tianna was oblivious to Tasha and Jamal's motives. She reluctantly agreed to his proposal to go bowling.

"What time should I pick you up?"

"How about seven?"

"All right, I will see you at seven. Oh, Tasha, I just saw your brother picking up some flowers from the flower shop. I asked who the lucky lady was, but he didn't say."

Tianna couldn't believe her ears. She cleared her throat and asked, "You saw Jackson? Where and when?"

Tasha and Jamal were taken aback at how Tianna asked about Jackson. She said it in an overly jealous way, as if Jackson was *her* man.

Jamal took the opportunity to start singing like a canary and told them the details of his encounter with Jackson.

After hearing that Jackson had flowers for some woman, Tianna was ready to go home. She lost her appetite and became moody and irritated. She wanted to pull her iPhone out of her purse and call him. She refrained, but it took massive willpower. She played her role like an Oscar award winner. She finished her conversation and outing with Tasha and Jamal like a good neighbor, but State Farm wasn't there. After hearing about Jackson buying flowers for another woman, she was going out with Jamal and couldn't wait.

Chapter Fourteen

"**S**trike," Tianna said as her bowling ball traveled down the lane.

"Lucky. Let's see you get another one." Jamal smirked.

Tianna wiggled her hips and batted her beady dark eyes as she reached for another bowling ball.

Jamal took everything in as he watched her hips, thighs, and of course her smile, and thought about how *lucky* he was to be with the woman he planned to make part of his future. He wanted to ask Tianna out again, and ask her to be his woman.

"Strikkkkeeeee!"

"Turkeyyyyy!" Tianna bragged about her three strikes in a row game.

Jamal quickly took the opportunity to grab Tianna and give her a kiss on the lips.

Tianna didn't object, in fact, his kiss took her back to the time in her room when they were in high school. The only difference was, this time Jamal's kiss was even better.

Jamal placed his arms around Tianna's waist and expressed how much fun he was having and thanked her for accepting his invitation to go bowling.

"Oh, don't be silly. You know I enjoy hanging with you."

"I know. You couldn't resist this charm and personality," Jamal said as he displayed his megawatt smile. His dark brown eyes did a samba dance in the bowling alley strobe lights. His brown skin was picture perfect without a single scar or pimple.

Jamal's bowling game was not as good as his basketball skills, but they didn't have to be.

His basketball skills were the blueprint to his career.

It wouldn't be long before he returned to school and entered the NBA draft.

Jamal had planned his life, and so far, everything was going as planned, except he hadn't made Tianna his girl, which would ensure she'd be his future wife.

Tianna and Jamal played a few more games before they left to get something to eat. They ate at a local restaurant before Tianna went home for the night.

Tianna went into her room but as soon as she undressed to take a shower, her cell phone rang.

It was Jackson probably asking about her whereabouts. He had been calling her for hours. Tianna had turned off her phone because she didn't want to hear from Mark. They'd had an argument the other night, and it was not their first. He was insecure and jealous and often accused Tianna of cheating on him. If Tianna's livelihood weren't tied to his family, she would have left Mark a long time ago. She had applied for many paid internships, but none had offered her an interview. She cared for Mark, but she didn't know if she *loved* him. They had many differences and they were coming full circle. Her return home for the holidays and seeing Jackson drove a bigger wedge in their fragile relationship.

After her shower and getting dressed, Tianna answered Jackson's call after the fourth ring. She was hesitant and really didn't feel like dealing with him. She'd had a great night with Jamal and wanted to take a shower and crawl into her bed for some much-needed rest.

"Hello," Tianna cooed into the phone.

"I've been calling you for hours. Where were you?"

"Umm, I don't get a hello, how are you, just attitude?"

"My bad, but yeah, how are you and where have you been? I've been so worried about you."

"Jackson, you don't have to protect me. I'm fine. I was out with a friend."

There was a knock on Tianna's bedroom door. It was her mother with a concerned look on her face, telling her some sad news about her father, Tyrone. He was hospitalized after passing out at work.

"Jackson, can I call you back?" Tianna asked.

"Sure, but I heard your mother. Do you want me to come take you to the hospital?"

"Umm, I don't know, but ummm, yes, that would be nice." Tianna couldn't think straight.

"All right. I'll be there." Jackson hung up the phone and was on his way to pick up Tianna.

He saw Tasha go into her room and didn't know whether to tell her about Tianna's father. He also didn't want her to know that he and Tianna had been secretly seeing one another. He decided against telling her, hurried out the front door, and got into this car to pick up Tianna.

Tianna and Jackson arrived at Methodist Hospital a short time later. They walked to the nurse's station to inquire about her father. The nurse knew Tianna because her mother Bernadette worked at the hospital. The nurse didn't ask Tianna for any identification, or if she was next of kin to Tyrone. She already knew that she was, so she directed Tianna to Tyrone's room. While walking down the hallway, Tianna noticed Tyrone's fiancée Stacy pacing the hall talking on her cellphone. She appeared distraught, but Tianna couldn't understand what she was saying. She asked how her father was, and Stacy couldn't talk. She continued crying hysterically.

"Tianna, he's not responsive and he's lost so much blood." Jackson placed his arms around Tianna to comfort her. She sobbed into his arms. She didn't really want to go inside the room to see her father. They didn't have a close relationship when she was younger, but they had begun to build a father and daughter relationship when Tianna graduated high school. She loved her father and wanted to continue to mend and build their relationship. She realized how young her father and mother were when she was conceived, and no longer blamed him for his immature ways. Her Deadbeat rhetoric subsided when they became closer. He began providing for her financially and mentally.

Tianna asked about her baby brother, T.J. She was informed that he was over at Stacy's sister's house while she stayed with Tyrone.

T.J was only three years old and Tianna and T.J were Tyrone's only children. Tianna wanted to see her brother to make sure that he was okay. But her primary concern was for her father. She mustered up enough strength to go in and see him.

Quietly, she knocked on the door and entered his room. Tyrone's mother Terrie was at his bedside reading scriptures from her King James Bible. Tianna and Jackson gave Terrie a hug. She didn't look up at them, she continued reading Bible verses and appeared to be in shock.

Tyrone was her only son. He was a mama's boy. Terrie had taken good care of him by working two jobs to make sure that he had everything he needed growing up. She did all that she could to supplement for the loss of his father, who passed away in a car accident when Tyrone was five years old. Terrie became a single mother raising her only son, and pregnant with Tyrone's sister Trina when their father was killed.

Trina was in the military and had been notified of her brother's condition. She was due to arrive the next morning from Denver, Colorado.

Tianna sat along the opposite side of Tyrone's bed and looked into his unresponsive face. She wanted to burst out crying, but held it together because of her grandmother. Her father didn't look anything like himself. The last time she saw him, he was laughing, healthy, and happy. He lay in the hospital bed with tubes coming out of his arms, nose, and mouth. He'd lost about twenty pounds and looked aged. He needed a haircut and a shave. His beard was fully gray and so was 75% of his hair. Tyrone was thirty-six years old, but looked about fifty-eight.

Tianna silently cried for her father as she held his hand. She prayed along with her grandmother for her father to return to himself. She laid her head on his shoulder. He didn't respond. He lay there like a vegetable. Tyrone had a stroke and fell from the second floor of a home he was constructing. He'd owned his own construction company since quitting high school when he inherited his grandfather's company. Tyrone had been going monthly for doctor visits after being diagnosed with sickle cell anemia, but he kept his diagnosis a secret. He didn't want to concern his mother or fiancée with his health issues, so he suffered in silence. He had been getting blood transfusions for almost a year, and had even been hospitalized because of the excruciating pain of the disease. This episode was more serious because he had a stroke and broke his leg and ribs in the fall.

Bernadette entered the room and offered to relieve Tianna from seeing her father in this condition. Tianna was happy to see her mother because she didn't want to see tubes going through her father nor hear the heart monitors that kept beeping every few seconds. Tyrone's breathing was shallow and faint. He was in critical condition and more serious than she knew.

Bernadette asked Jackson to take Tianna home and told her she would call her if his condition changed for the better or worse.

Jackson did what he was told and took Tianna home.

Jackson walked Tianna to her room and sat on the bed holding her in his arms. She was able to release the cries that she'd held inside at the hospital. She cried in Jackson's arms and he held her tight. He undressed her, gave her a nightie, and tucked her into bed.

He lay right next to her, holding and comforting her as she fell into a deep slumber. Tianna slept as her cell phone rang with Mark's name displayed on the screen.

Jackson wanted to answer to curse Mark out and tell him to never call his woman again. He was concerned for Tianna, and Mark calling her every hour on the hour was not only getting on Tianna's nerves, but Jackson's as well.

Jackson retrieved Tianna's phone that read ten missed calls.

When Jackson set the phone on the nightstand, it began to ring again.

Jackson pushed the green answer button.

"Yeah," he hissed as he walked out of Tianna's room, trying not to wake her.

"Who the hell is this?"

"Who the hell are you!" Jackson retorted.

"Where is Tianna?" Mark asked.

"She's busy and don't call this phone anymore," Jackson said and hung up.

Mark was beyond pissed. He was determined to know who answered Tianna's phone, so he called back several times.

Jackson didn't answer. Instead, he sent Mark straight to voicemail where he left many angry voice messages.

Jackson turned off Tianna's phone. He went back to her bedroom, lay next to her, and drifted off to sleep.

Chapter Fifteen

Bernadette entered Tyrone's room to check his vital signs. She witnessed Tyrone's mother and fiancée in the corner of the room asleep in La-Z-Boy recliner chairs. They had been at the hospital for twenty-four hours without sleep. Bernadette was as quiet as possible, trying not to wake them. She lifted Tyrone's left arm and that's when she realized there was no pulse or movement in his body. She panicked, but tried to remain calm. She couldn't believe the heart rate monitor didn't go off. She ran to the nurse's station to get Dr. Ramsey. He was with another patient, but came as soon as Bernadette set off the code blue alert. Dr. Ramsey immediately entered Tyrone's room. He turned on the lights and awakened everyone. He apologized and asked Terrie and Stacy to please leave the room.

Bernadette helped calm Terrie down. She wanted to know what was going on.

Stacy began to cry out loud, "Oh My God! He's not breathing. Tyrone, baby wake up!"

Another nurse came to intervene and assisted Terrie and Stacy out of the room. She knew how serious the matter was and knew that Dr. Ramsey needed help.

Dr. Ramsey checked Tyrone's vitals, but there were none.

Tyrone lay there cold and stiff, rigor mortis had already set in, so he had to have died at least an hour or more ago. There was no need to do CPR because he was dead. But why didn't the heart rate monitor alarm them?

Dr. Ramsey turned to Bernadette to say how sorry he was for her loss. Bernadette held it together the best that she could, but ran inside the bathroom to cry for Tyrone.

How was she going to tell Tianna that her father was dead? She and Tyrone had their disagreements, but she still loved him. *He was her child's father*.

Dr. Ramsey pronounced Tyrone dead and asked for the nurse to clean him and then contact the morgue. He would talk to the family that was awaiting Tyrone's fate.

Dr. Ramsey walked into the waiting room to deliver the sad news, but when Terrie saw the look on his face, she knew that her son was dead.

"No, I don't want to hear it. Don't say it, doctor. I'm supposed to die *before* my child."

"I'm sorry, Mrs. Jones."

"No, not my baby. My baby ain't dead," Terrie said as she tried to get inside the room to see her son.

"Mrs. Jones, please, we will let you in to see him, but he's deceased. I'm sorry."

"Whatttt? Oh, my God! Mama, tell me my brother is not dead!" Trina said, finally arriving at the hospital, just in time to witness Dr. Ramsey delivering the bad news about Tyrone.

Bernadette came out of the bathroom to take a final look at Tyrone. She kissed his cheek and whispered, "Rest easy. I'll see you in the other world."

She walked outside the room to see Stacy and Trina crying hysterically. She comforted Trina. The other nurse, Maggie, comforted Stacy, and Dr. Ramsey was with Terrie, trying to console her.

"What am I going to do without him? How am I going to tell our son, T.J. that his father is dead?" Stacy asked herself.

All that could be heard were cries and apologies coming from the family and the hospital staff.

"Why didn't the heart monitor sound?" Terrie kept asking Dr. Ramsey.

He couldn't answer but was having a staff member look into the possible malfunction.

"They done killed my, baby!" Terrie cried.

Tyrone Jones was deceased at the age of thirty-six.

Chapter Sixteen

Tianna was on her way back home to Boston. Her father was buried and she'd said her goodbyes to family and friends. It was time to get back to work. She mourned her father and felt conflicted because he wasn't in her life until high school. Her grief for Tyrone was more about her little brother and mother. She would miss her father and the relationship that they were building, but she was indifferent about his death. His life was so short that she didn't really get a chance to know him.

Tianna didn't want to leave her family or Jackson, but she knew that she had to return. If not, she would never go back to school. She had unfinished business to attend to, and as soon as she was finished with school, she would be moving home to Texas.

Mark picked Tianna up from the airport but the encounter was not very warm. They were a happy couple before the trip to her hometown, but her time away had strained their relationship.

Mark reached over to give Tianna a hug and a kiss, and whispered how much he missed her. Tianna returned the embrace, but it was not sincere. She remembered some of the mean remarks Mark had made over the phone during their arguments. He had never talked to her that way before and she didn't know what to expect from him upon her return. His loving demeanor caught her by surprise. He gave his condolences for her father and even offered to fly to the funeral when she was away. Tianna asked that he not come and said she would be returning home to Boston the next day. He accepted without a fight and respected her wishes.

"My parents send their condolences to you and said that it's all right if you take more time off work for bereavement."

"No, I'll be fine. Work is something that I need to get my mind off everything. Thank you, though."

"No, problem, babe, you know that I'm here for you."

"Thanks. I know," Tianna said as she stroked Mark's right arm to show her appreciation.

"Are you hungry, you want to go to dinner?"

"Thanks, I have jet lag and just want to get some rest. I will take a rain check."

Mark tried not to show his disappointment over being turned down for dinner, or how much he wanted to spend time with his woman. He felt the emotional detachment he has been getting from Tianna since her vacation. He didn't know if it was the "right time" to bring his emotions into play since Tianna just lost her father.

He opened Tianna's front door and walked her inside. .

Pauline couldn't believe her eyes when she saw Tianna walk into the apartment.

"Errk, where have you been?" she asked, and didn't wait for an answer when she began her, "Tianna loves Jackson" rant.

Mark gasped and told Pauline to get quiet before he threw her out.

"Errk, try it," Pauline said.

Mark went to the cage and began shaking it as though he was getting ready to throw her out the window.

Tianna asked Mark to stop because she really wasn't in the mood and just wanted to get some rest. Mark asked if she wanted him to stay and rub her feet. She politely declined and issued another rain check.

She kissed Mark goodnight and he left.

Tianna went into her room to turn on the television. She disrobed and turned on the shower. She never took a shower without her music, so while showering, the Hot 97 radio station played Oldies-but-Goodies, and Aalyah's, "Let Me Know" played through the speakers.

Tianna began to sing and reminisce about Jackson and their last night together. It had been special. Jackson got down on one knee to propose to her. She accepted his proposal, but postponed the wedding until after graduation. She was taking eighteen credit hours per semester, so she was due to graduate early.

It was official; Jackson and Tianna were secretly engaged. Tianna didn't know how to tell Tasha or Mark. She cared for them and didn't want to hurt either, but she couldn't put her happiness on hold to please others. She didn't want to lose her best friend, but she decided that she must follow her heart. And her heart was with Jackson.

Jamal was at Tianna's father's funeral and he came by her mother's home afterwards. He and Tianna talked and he confessed his love for her and told her that he would be entering the NBA draft next season and that he wanted to take her with him. Tianna was in disbelief and honored. She didn't tell Jamal that she was already engaged to Jackson. She didn't want them fighting, nor was it the time or place. She didn't give Jamal a "yes" or a "no," she gave him an "undecided." It was as if she was stringing him along.

Tasha, as resilient as she could be, surprised everyone by showing them a day before the funeral that she could walk without assistance, and how she practiced in her bedroom each night to get back to the way she was before the accident.

She promised Tianna a visit to Boston during spring break and Tianna took her up on her offer. During her visit she would tell Tasha about her relationship with Jackson. She prayed that her friend would understand and that she wouldn't end their friendship.

Tianna pondered how to end the relationship with Mark and how her livelihood would be affected since she worked at his parents' law firm.

She thought about looking for another job as early as tomorrow morning.

Mark waited outside Tianna's apartment before driving off. He heard a ding sound and tried to pinpoint where it was coming from. He checked his phone and nothing.

The ding sound continued as Mark reached under his passenger's seat and found Tianna's iPhone. She must've left it in his car. He tried not to read her messages, but couldn't help it when he saw Jackson's name and contact information.

He thought to himself, *so this is Jackson?*
This is the mothersucker who has my girl's heart?
Well, let's see what Jackson has to say...

Mark unlocked Tianna's phone because he insisted one day that she give him the passcode to prove her loyalty to him.

Jackson: Hey, babe, I hope you made it home safe. Give me a call when you get home.
Jackson: I can't wait to see you, again
Jackson: I love you.

Mark was livid! He turned off the car engine and got out the car, walked to Tianna's font door, and began banging on it.

Dogs were barking and neighbor's lights began to pop on.

"Tianna, open the goddamn door," Mark yelled.

Tianna was deep in her music and couldn't hear Mark banging on the door.

The dog barking got louder.

"Shut up, you mutts!" Mark screamed at the barking dogs to no avail. They continued barking.

Tianna couldn't hear Mark because she was too busy thinking about her fiancé and how she was going to break the news to Mark that it was over.

Bam, Bam, Bam

"Tianna!" he called out.

Mark went around the back of the apartment and retrieved the spare key hidden in the secret place under the trash can.

He walked to the front of the apartment, unlocked the door, and entered unannounced.

Pauline began cursing Mark out.

"Errk, why the hell are you so loud and what are you doing here? I'm trying to sleep, you fool. Get the hell out of here!"

Mark ignored Pauline. His focus was on Tianna.

"Tianna, where the hell are you?" Mark continued to call, searching the kitchen and then going upstairs to her bedroom.

He went into Tianna's room and heard the radio and shower, and Tianna singing.

He opened the bathroom door and grabbed her out of the shower.

"Mark, noooooooooo!!" Tianna cried.

Chapter Seventeen

*D*ear Diary,

I've been feeling nauseous for over three months. It's finally spring break and Tasha will be here tonight. I must clean the apartment and get myself together. I've been working long hours at the law firm and haven't had time to do anything, let alone clean.

It seems like I have gained at least ten pounds. I need to get a membership at Gold's Gym to work off these extra pounds.

I haven't spoken to Mark all week, and to be honest, I'd like to keep it that way. I've been looking for internships since the New Year, but nothing. I have to keep applying because I want out!

Tianna's phone rang, but she thought it was the morning alarm clock awaking her. She reached to the nightstand to click the snooze button, but the ring continued.

Tianna placed the comforter over her head to muffle the sound of the ring.

It stopped momentarily and then started again.

Tianna's doorbell rang and she got up to see who was at the door. She looked through the peephole and it was Tasha!

What is she doing here? She isn't supposed to be here until later tonight. The apartment is a mess. I'm a mess, Tianna thought to herself.

"Tianna, Girlllll, open this door. It's Tasha!"

Should I let my best friend continue to knock and pretend I'm not here or open the door and let her see me and my apartment this way?

Tianna pondered. She couldn't decide.

Tianna went back to her room to put on her robe and Spongebob house slippers she'd had since she was a little girl.

She opened the door and couldn't believe her eyes. It was Tasha *and* Jackson!

"Girl, what took you so long? Who's in here with you?" Tasha asked. She did a search of the apartment as soon as she stepped over the threshold.

"Yeah, tell that Negro I said get the gettin' because Jackson is here."

"Did you forget to clean? You knew I was coming, right?"

"Hey guys, I'm so sorry. I thought you were coming in later tonight and I've been so busy with work and school, I haven't had time to clean," Tianna explained.

"Well, if I'm going to be here for a week then I can't stay in this dumpster fire. You know I'm a neat freak, so I'm going to help you clean right now. Where is the Lysol spray?" Tasha asked.

"Hi Pauline, I have heard so much about you. I'm glad to finally meet you," she said as she walked passed the parrot's cage.

"Tianna loves Jackson."

"What?"

Tianna, and Jackson busted out laughing watching Tasha's reaction to Pauline.

"Y'all don't pay Pauline any mind. Pauline, meet Tasha and Jackson."

"Errkk, nice to meet you. Tianna loves Jackson."

"Oh, she does, huh?" Jackson asked Pauline.

"Pauline, you want a muzzle?"

"Errrk, I won't say another word."

"She's adorable. I want a parrot," Tasha said. "But I don't want it telling my business."

Tasha asked Jackson to take their luggage to the guestroom and told him he would be on the sofa for the entire week while she occupied the guest bed. Jackson sighed and did what he was asked. As he was on his way to the guestroom, and Tasha was nowhere in sight because she was looking for cleaning supplies, he grabbed Tianna and gave her a sensual hug and kiss. It didn't matter about her morning breath because that's how much he loved her.

He whispered how much he missed her and couldn't wait to get back to where they'd left off over the Christmas holidays. He grabbed her ass and asked her to point him to the guest bedroom. She smiled and personally took him there.

Tianna unlocked the guestroom door and showed Jackson where to put the luggage. Jackson closed and locked the door, and pulled her close.

"Man, I miss you so much. I hope you didn't mind your fiancé coming along with Tasha. She told me of her plans to visit and I took vacation time to come along. I just had to see you."

"No, it's fine. I was just surprised and caught off guard. Look at me. I'm a mess and so is my apartment."

"Ahh, don't worry about it. Tasha will have this place cleaned in no time. You know how she gets down."

"Yeah, I know, but it's not her job to clean up after me. I was planning to clean and get ready to pick her up at the airport later tonight."

"Yo, you feeling okay? I see you put on a little weight back there," Jackson said as he continued to hold and feel all over her perfect figure.

Tianna explained that she'd been nauseated, and eating and working a lot, but that she was fine. She wanted to get a membership at the gym to keep her weight down. She explained how she was seeking new employment and told him about how school was going and how much she needed this break. She wanted to relax and go wherever Tasha wanted while she was in Boston. Jackson asked if she'd broken things off with Mark since they were engaged, and she explained to him that she was in the process, but she hadn't found a job, yet, and that working at the firm paid her bills. He said that he could take care of her and that she really didn't need to work at the firm. He had money saved. He was still in pharmacy school, but he was a trust fund baby and received an inheritance from his grandmother.

"Baby, I got you. You're going to be my wife. I want you to come back home with me."

"Jackson, I know, but I have to finish school first. It won't be long until we spend the rest of our lives, together," Tianna said as she puckered her lips and batted her eyes. The sight of her doing that drove him crazy.

Tianna told Jackson that she needed to go shower and he asked if he could go with her and that he needed a shower, too. She pushed him down on the bed and straddled him. She wished that they were alone because she would have taken him up on the offer.

She kissed him again before she left him in the guestroom.

As she left the room, she bumped into Tasha.

"Tianna, what are you and my brother up to?"

"Nothing, why do you ask?"

"Hmmm, mmmm, something is up with you, two. Why he would want to come with me to Boston is beyond me."

"Girl, let me go get cleaned up and I will talk to you later."

"Yeah, I see you put on a little weight. Mark must be treating you well. When will I meet him?"

"Soon," Tianna said.

"I better. You've been saying that for the longest time. Is he ugly and that's why I haven't met him? If so, it's okay, because ugly men need love, too."

"Tasha, you stupid. Mark is not *ugly*. Trust me."

They both laughed as Tianna briskly walked to her room to get into the shower and Tasha followed. She told Tasha she would be ready in a little bit and would help clean the apartment.

"We can order pizza and watch movies for today and then go paint the town tomorrow."

"That's cool, but we need to stop at the drugstore tonight to get a pregnancy test because you have gained too much weight and I'm getting a pregnancy vibe from you."

"Pregnant? Tasha, I am not pregnant. I'm just stressed and overworked."

"Yeah, okay. Whatever you say. I need to meet this Mark fellow."

"Byeeee, Tasha."

Hours later, the apartment was sparkling clean and so was Tianna. She looked scrumptious and Jackson could hardly keep his eyes off his fiancée. Whenever Tasha got up to leave the room, they were all over each other, and when she returned, they'd pretended like nothing happened.

The doorbell rang and Jackson went to the door to answer and pay the pizza man.

He didn't know how much to tip him because it had been at least an hour since they ordered two large pizzas. One pizza was a supreme and the other was a veggie.

Jackson opened the door and there stood a gentleman with no pizza.

"Yo, what's up man, where's the pizza?"

"Pizza, what pizza?"

"We ordered pizza, so I was expecting the delivery man. Who are you?"

"None of your business. Where's Tianna?" Mark stepped inside the apartment uninvited.

"Tianna, Tianna. Where are you sweetie?" he called.

"Wait a minute. Who the fuck are you?"

Tasha and Tianna heard voices coming from the doorway and they both got up to see what was going on, and why Jackson was taking so long with the pizzas.

Tianna gasped when she saw Mark inside the apartment calling her name.

"Oh, there you are, dear. Who are these people?"

"Tianna loves Jackson," Pauline said in the background.

She had been quiet all day.

"Tianna, who is this white boy?" Tasha asked with a confused look on her face.

"Yeah, who is this white boy about to get his ass beat?" Jackson said with venom in his voice.

"I'm Mark, Tianna's boyfriend."

"What the hell!"

"Tianna's boyfriend?" Tasha said as she held her mouth in shock and turned toward Tianna to see her reaction and wait for her to explain.

Tianna cleared her throat and introduced everyone.

Jackson was hot as cayenne pepper. He began cracking his knuckles to keep from cracking Mark upside his head.

Tasha stood there speechless with her mouth opened. She had never known Tianna to be attracted to white guys. She took a sip of her Fuji water and took a seat on the sofa to watch the show.

"Mark, have a seat. Everyone, calm down and chill out!" Tianna raised her voice over all the commotion. She couldn't handle the back and forth exchange of words between her fiancé and her soon-to-be ex-boyfriend.

"Calm down?. What the hell you mean, calm down, Tianna?!"

"Jackson, please let me explain."

"Errrrk, Tianna loves Jackson," Pauline called out.

"Shut up, Pauline!" Everyone said in unison.

Tasha stood next to her brother trying to understand why he was so mad at Mark and Tianna. She wondered if it was more than Mark's race that bothered him.

"Jackson, this is between Tianna and Mark, you need to let them handle this. It has nothing to do with you."

"Like hell it don't! Tell them, Tianna, or else I will!"

"Tell us what?"

"Yeah, tell us what?" Mark asked.

They all watched Tianna as she struggled to tell everyone about her secret relationship with Jackson. Not only about their affair, but that they were engaged. She was planning to leave Mark and marry Jackson after graduation. But she still hadn't found a job and was working for Mark's parents at their law firm. She knew that once she ended the relationship with Mark, her employment ended as well.

Tianna couldn't speak. She acted as though the cat cut off her tongue and it lay next to her bleeding to death. She had her head down and fidgeted from side to side.

"You know what? I don't have time for this! I'm outta here," Jackson said as he grabbed his leather coat and rental car keys and stomped out the door.

"Jackson, where are you going?" Tasha called.

He said nothing, as if he didn't hear her. He didn't even look back.

The only thing they heard were the squealing tires of a pissed off man behind the wheel.

Tears began to overflow on Tianna's face, but still, no words could be heard. She looked at Tasha and mumbled, "I'm sorry."

"Mark, can I please talk with you privately in my room?"

Tianna went to her room and Mark followed, becoming angrier.

She knew how he got when he was angry, and she wanted to tame his outburst, but not in front of Tasha. She didn't want anyone to know that he had been abusing her since they met.

"Mark, I'm sorry. I didn't mean to hurt you."

"What do you mean? Tianna what are you talking about."

"I'm in love…"

Instantly, Mark slapped Tianna across her face. He picked up the vase from her nightstand. He hit her across her face with the vase and continued to beat her with it until it broke.

Tasha banged on the door trying to get inside, but the door was locked. "Tianna, open the door, now!"

But Tianna couldn't because she was unconscious, lying on the floor, bleeding from her head, mouth, nose, and everywhere.

Mark went into a rage. He picked Tianna up and threw her back on the floor.

"You black bitch!" he said over and over between each punch. "I should have left you in the ghetto."

Tasha picked up her cell phone to dial 911.

But the beating continued for what seemed like five minutes before Mark opened the door and left.

He walked past Tasha with a pocket knife in his hand and it was covered in blood.

Tasha was hysterical and thankful that she heard sirens in the distance because she could have been next.

She went into the room to find Tianna's limp body on the floor, and screamed. "Oh my God! Somebody, help!"

Thank you for reading and please stay tuned for Tar Baby 2 in May 2019.

Please rate and leave a review on Amazon or Goodreads. I would appreciate it.